MW00886276

PRAISE FOR SUSAN TROTT'S NOVELS

"Trott breaks a lot of literary rules but is able to get away with it because of her dynamic writing style. *Divorcing Daddy* is funny from beginning to end and guarantees a laugh at least every ten minutes." Rocky Mountain News

"Susan Trott is a master at revealing madness in the mundane as well as lucidity in the lunacy of our lives. This skill, combined with a keen yet sensitive eye for human self-deception, makes for a fun, refreshing and ultimately enlightening read."
Bloomsbury Review

"Susan Trott has such an individual style that she is practically a genre unto herself. Her heroines find adventure entwined with menace, freedom flirting with obsession, passion courting chaos and, always, love a possibility."
San Francisco Chronicle

When Your Lover Leaves... "I loved the heroine, her humor, her courage and her genuine goodness. I very much admire Susan Trott for bringing her to life."
Anne Tyler

Sightings: "Trott displays a sensitivity to human quirkiness and longings that make this a splendid entertainment." The New York Times Book Review

"A marvelously entertaining novel. The ending is lovely and haunting ... a peculiarly satisfying story." Washington Post Book World

"As a writer, Susan Trott isn't like anybody else. She is funny, willful, insouciant and original. Clearly she has a love for words and can make the language hum."
Chicago Tribune

"The writing is catchy and sophisticated. Trott catches her setting with an eerie lyricism. Washington Post

"*Sightings* is full of symbolism, of history nearly repeating itself, of magical revelations. There is love, despair, pathos and powerful writing that will leave the reader breathless." Richmond Times-Dispatch.

Pursued By the Crooked Man: "Susan Trott does not fit neatly into any category, her voice is uniquely her own. She often writes about betrayal and how it is embedded in the very nature of love. Her world is boldly and imaginatively drawn."
Los Angeles Times Book Review

The Housewife and the Assassin zooms along at a breakneck pace. Her ending is a surprising salute to the power wielded by human emotions."
Little Rock Arkansas

"Susan Trott seems to know exactly what she's doing and how to go about it. Her book is skillfully entertaining – and she understands male psychology, which is rather alarming."
Evan S. Connell

"If you have ever run for sport or for your life, you might recognize the author's fantasies about death and legging go as your own." Michael Murphy

"The writing is fresh, amusing, inventive, and constantly surprising."
Chicago Tribune Book World

"It is a fine novel, perceptive and very sensual." Santa Rosa Press Democrat

"In Susan Trott's novel, descriptions are beautiful, no words are wasted, and the story moves along in an intriguing way. I found it difficult to put the book down."
The South Bend Indiana Tribune

Crane Spreads Wings, A bigamist's Story: "This madcap exploration of love and art is sure to win Trott new readers with its unpretentious, breezy appeal." Publishers Weekly

"Trott has learned how to present sharply drawn characters who are complex and thoughtful as well as amusing. She can sketch minor characters in a brief exchange of dialogue, yet she can also take time to provide lyrical descriptions while keeping her intricate plot moving swiftly and surely." The New York Times Book Review

"Crane Spreads Wings is Trott at her finest – funny touching memorable." Lynn Freed.

"Trott is one of my favorite writers. And what a novel twist on the classic human dilemma – love, loss, love." Anne Lamott

Trott's novels are always a journey or a least a trip, that connects her unique charm and light-hearted wisdom." Martin Cruz Smith

"The writing sparkles. The effect is lyrical and charming." Philidelphia Inquirer

Also by Susan Trott

The Housewife and the Assassin

When Your Lover Leaves ...

Incognito

Don't Tell Laura

Sightings

Pursued by the Crooked Man

The Exception

Divorcing Daddy

The Holy Man

Tainted Million

The Holy Man's Journey

Crane Spreads Wings, a bigamist's story

The Holy Woman

For Children

Mr. Privacy

The Sea Serpent of Horse

FLAMINGO THIEF

BY

SUSAN TROTT

© 2010 Susan Trott. All rights reserved

ISBN 978-0-557-65228-0

www.LuLu.com
ID 9314770

"Out beyond ideas of wrong doing and right doing, there is a field. I will meet you there." Rumi

FLAMINGO THIEF

PART ONE — FLAMINGO THEFTS

PART TWO — FLAMINGO RETURNS

PART ONE

FLAMINGO THEFTS

I

FIRST FLAMINGO

I was playing with my three year old niece, Joy, when I stole the first flamingo. My hands looked destructive and colossal in the little dollhouse, which she populated with china animals instead of dolls.

"You be the puppy and me be the tiger, horse, and coyote." With a decisive look, she took up these animals in her little hands, pushing back her flyaway strands of reddish hair. She had the look and personality of a tough, little, Irish kid from her mother's side of the family, but was also sensitive, sweet, and dreamy from her Uncle Tim's side, Uncle Tim being me.

"Why do you get to be three animals and I only get to be one?" I asked plaintively.

"'Cause you're the puppy. That's the best."

I knew that in her dollhouse world, the puppy was the prime animal, alpha male. I commenced making puppy sounds, which she had taught me to do the last time we played china animals. She roared and neighed and howled, chasing poor puppy around the dollhouse, in and out of rooms, up and down stairs. Out on the roof was allowed, too, despite questionable egress. The puppy always out-foxed the other animals, or out-puppied them, as I'd taught Joy to say. We learned from each other.

"Tim!" called Laurie, Joy's mother. "Don't let Joy commandeer you. We want you with us."

"Five minutes!" I called back

In the dollhouse bathroom I discovered, and was mesmerized by, a china flamingo about an inch high, bright pink, lying on its side. I stood it

up. Something about it made me feel happy, seemed to uncork some flamingo memory from my youth despite my hailing from Maine, a flamin-
goless state if there ever was one, no pink to be had anywhere, any season.
Maine was like an old black and white movie. It was something about the
pink color itself that pleased me so immoderately, although the tiny bird
was charming.

"I miss Jamie," Joy said. She always talked about Jamie when we
played together and I loved it that she did. No one else did, thinking, I suppose, to spare me, but instead only making me feel more abandoned. Even
his mother, Stella, didn't talk about him.

"I miss him, too, Joy, honey."

"What is dying?"

"I don't know how it was for Jamie. I hope it was nice   For me, it is
not having him around anymore. It is Jamie being gone forever and it is
horrible."

"Howible," Joy agreed, or she could have been correcting my pronun-
ciation.

Stella came into the playroom. She wore white linen slacks and a
black V-neck jersey with silver jewelry. From where I was crouched on the
floor, she looked tall and exotically thin, like a dancer. Her black hair
touched her shoulders, the kind of hair that moved, that she could run her
fingers through and it would fall back into place and shine outrageously.
When she was in school, girls would ask her what product she used to
make it shine and she told them shoe polish, which was mean because they
all tried it. Now, at thirty-seven, women still envied her hair and men
wanted to touch it, grab it, grab her.

"Joy," she said kindly. "We have to take Tim away from you. It's dinner time."

2

"Does Uncle Tim have to eat tonight?"

While Stella talked to Joy, I took the flamingo. I nabbed it. My fingers, as if acting wholly on their own, tucked it into the small pocket on the front of my jeans, the watch pocket. Perfect fit. Flamingo pocket.

"See you later, Uncle Tim."

"Before then, I hope."

As I entered the dining room, my brother, George, was bragging about me to the other couple he and Laurie had invited to dinner, two doctors, Marie and Alvin Stein. George was a doctor also, an anesthesiologist. He was blond, like me, but shorter, heavier, with a strangely dark mustache. Laurie was a lawyer, currently being a mom. She was big and strong, a golfer, tall and thin like me, but with bigger biceps. The Steins were exceedingly small and she was French. My beloved Stella was an artist.

"Here he is now, the King of Juice!" George threw an arm around me. He was indefatigably proud of me even though my success was luck and timing. He was the hard-working, smart brother.

"It all started with a lemonade stand when Tim was a kid. He insisted on using real lemons. No frozen or canned stuff. He set up his stand by a creek, had a hand squeezer, and he diluted the lemon juice with creek water which, a man ahead of his time even then, he called pure mountain spring water."

"It really was ..."

"Shut up, kid, this is my story." Still with his arm around me he kissed me on the cheek, showing his love. "When he came to California, he discovered oranges in a big way, grapefruit, too. At college, his room was full of electric juicers and he sold bottles of juice around the dorms."

"Don't tell the whole story," Stella begged. "Just go direct to the fame and fortune part: Zeus Juice."

3

"So you are Zeus Juice," said Marie in her sexy French accent. "My fridge is completely full of it. Tasty!"

"Now he uses fruit like kumquats and loquats that no one ever heard of," George said. "Kiwi and weewee."

George was drunk, bless him. "My weewee juice is particularly popular," I said modestly.

"And he has just expanded out of state," he went on, busting with pride, although without his initial investment I wouldn't have expanded out of the garage where Zeus began.

"Of course he could make even more money selling water but he didn't have the vision. Who would have thought water would sell?"

My mind wandered from my fame and fortune to my recent degradation. I just stole a china animal from a child, I told myself, and felt a blush of shame.

"You're embarrassing him, George," Laurie said. "Enough. Sit down everyone. Let's eat."

Laurie: goodhearted, earnest, down-to-earth, often had to pull George back down to earth, or at least into his chair.

During dinner, I felt the flamingo in my pocket pressing against my stomach. I wanted it and I took it. I had never stolen anything in my life and now I had stolen from my own, dear niece. It both pleased and horrified me. I knew something about myself that none of my intimates knew. What I didn't know was why I had done it. Joy would have given it to me if I had asked. But I wanted to steal it and I did.

Everyone toasted me happy birthday. Laurie had baked a fabulous cake. There were thirty-nine candles including the one to grow on, which I set aside in a dish while I blew out the others. If it burned down it meant I would live out the year, but it didn't.

4

"It's a stupid custom," Laurie said, upset.

"My candles to-grow-on always go out," I assured her. "But I always grow on. I would worry if the flame burned down. It's a reverse-luck thing with me."

"We do not do this in France," said Marie.

"It's not a Jewish thing," said Alvin.

"I wonder where it does come from," said Stella. "Not Mexico."

Driving home to Sausalito, I interrupted Stella's gossipy commentary on the party to ask, "Why don't we have anything pink in our house?"

"Because it's an awful color."

Stella used cool colors in her paintings and her content was cool: a slightly ruined book lying on a table, a vase of dying flowers, a torn curtain hanging lifeless at an open window, a wine glass with a glimmer of wine at the bottom — but not waiting to be finished or refilled because the contents had not been relished to begin with — or because it was a dirty glass, unwashed for days. One felt, something unexpected had happened. There was ever this faint aura of dread, which belied the cheerful person she was, or used to be. However, her paintings were gloomy even before Jamie died.

We were both happy-go-lucky people before we lost our son almost a year ago and still appeared as such. Smilers. Laughers. We had the world on a string. Now the string was frayed to breaking, but we soldiered on, going by memory of how to appear happy. The facial muscles remembered how to smile and the laughs rang out as of yore only sometimes getting cramped in the throat midway, turning into a coughing fit or crying fit.

We parked in the lot and walked the hundred yards down the dock to our deep-water houseboat. It was a warm July night, but there was a breeze. I touched the flamingo through the denim as if it were a talisman. It made me feel genuinely glad.

Or stealing it did. Or the pink …

"Don't you love the dock at night, the shimmering lights reflecting in the water. This is heaven. Aren't you glad we moved, Tim?"

"Yes," I lied. Stella had wanted to sell the Mill Valley house where every inch contained a memory of Jamie. It tore her up to be there. But I loved it. I loved every inch of memory. Yes, the houseboat was beautiful and romantic, but there was no Jamie there anywhere. I felt that selling the house was a big mistake. So I didn't. I kept it. I could go there whenever I wanted to even though it wasn't the same without our furniture. Stella didn't know. George knew. After a while, when I felt ready I would sell it to just the right little family, maybe.

Everyone deals with death in his or her own way. I respected Stella's ways. It was easy to give in to her wishes and secretly carry out my wishes.

One thinks of houseboats as charming, quirky abodes, something out of a children's book, and some of them on the dock were: transformed tug boats, pieced-together cottages floating on concrete hulls, roomy old barges, ferry boats turned into apartments, Dutch canal boats, even a Spanish galleon. But ours was brand new, a modern architectural marvel, mostly glass, with high beamed ceilings, skylights, maple floors, granite fireplace and counters, sliding doors opening to various decks and balconies, a view of the wide lagoon, of Mount Tamalpais, and a big sky without telephone wires. All this nature was ours with San Francisco only ten miles away. Stella had filled planters with yellow and red roses, jasmine vines, and bougainvillea. When it came to flowers, she let her colors get hot. Except for pink.

We went directly downstairs. In the master bedroom, Stella flung off her clothes and went into the movie-star bathroom/spa, all marble and mirrors. I went down the hall to undress in my accustomed way then, returning to the bedroom, I dropped down the curtains. The room was messy as if the contents of her paintings had been joined together to make a room: the flung clothes, coffee cups and glasses, stacks of books, paintings by friends hanging helter-skelter on the walls. But all this looked warm and colorful and joyful instead of abandoned, shadowy, eerie as they did when captured on her canvasses.

As it was my birthday, Stella said I could ask anything of her and I did. Nice present. But it was not that different from other nights. She was a generous lover, a sexy woman, and the fact we'd been married a hundred years, well, almost twenty, made no difference to our desire for each other, only enhanced it, for me anyhow. She spoke love words to me in Spanish. It was like singing: soft, tuneful, and sweet.

"Please stay," she said afterward, her face between my shoulder and neck, breath warm, hair silken.

"I have to …"

"I know, but …"

"I'll come back."

"It's not the same."

But in a minute she was asleep. She sometimes fell asleep mid-sentence. It was a gift.

Quietly, I got up and stepped down the hall, past doors hiding laundry, furnace, hot water heater, sewage holding tank, to the guest room, my room. Before joining Stella in bed, I had put the little flamingo on my bedside table, the inch-high statue becoming the one non-furniture item in the Spartan room, and I had laid out fresh clothes for the morning: a white button-down shirt, dark blue sweater, faded 501 jeans, paraboots. I had put today's shirt in the laundry bag, the other clothes in the washer.

In bed I told Jamie about my birthday, aloud, which is why I couldn't go to sleep with Stella next to me. She couldn't stand hearing me talking to him and I couldn't go to sleep without doing so.

"I went to the office today, not the shop. The office is full of all these new idiots. I think one had blow-dried hair, another a perm, even though we are talking men here. The idea is to hire marketing people and financial gurus to launch Zeus Juice out of state, into the new millennium and thence to the stratosphere, but these men are not like you and I, James, not like your Uncle George."

Everyone called him Jamie so James was my nickname for him. He loved it that I called him James. It was only when we were alone together. Then he would call me Father instead of Dad. Or Sir. We thought it was terribly funny.

I went on to tell about my birthday at George and Laurie's, playing with Joy, how she had asked about him. I only touched briefly on the flamingo theft, glancing over it, saying, "Joy had this tiny flamingo. Now it is here on my bedside table next to the clock, being an ornament for my austere room, creating a whole new mini-atmosphere.

"Goodnight, James," I said at the end, "I love you."

Now I could travel back down the hall and sleep with Stella but the litany of speaking to my son relaxed me, eased me into sleep, and it would all be lost if I got up. It would all be ruined. And sleep was so desirable, such a release, the only reprieve, the only nepenthe.

It was quiet except for lone footsteps tip-tapping down the wooden dock. Beams from a dock light came through where the curtains met and traveled across the small room to my bedside table to illuminate the blob

8

of stolen pink. My eyelids closed, the pink stayed behind them a moment, then faded out,

II

FLAMINGO DAGWOOD

About ten days later, when I stole the second flamingo, it took me by surprise. There was nothing further from my mind. Well, the first flamingo was a surprise, too, but ...

Anyhow, I never expected to steal another, maybe because I didn't expect to see another. The places I went, the things that I did, the people I saw, didn't include china flamingoes. But it is like any oddball thing — you see it for the first time, notice it, and soon you see it again.

Why did I steal it? Why didn't I ask for it or buy it? I don't know — maybe because the stealing moved my blood, made me feel alive, the part of me that had died with Jamie.

I helicoptered to and from work that day. Although Zeus' offices were in nearby San Rafael, the plant where the juice was squeezed and bottled, mostly by Mexican employees, was forty miles away in Vallejo. The heliport was only a mile from our dock and I could walk to it along the shore bike path. Being in a residential area (the houseboat community was seven docks in all, about five hundred floating homes), the heliport was only granted six take-offs and landings a day, but I had an arrangement with them and they could usually count me in. They had two sea planes as well which I could also hire in a pinch as Vallejo was on San Pablo Bay, a northeasterly extension of San Francisco Bay, with Sausalito's (our) little Richardson Bay taking a dip between the two huge ones.

Marine World USA was in Vallejo and Zeus Juice was near enough that I could, did, used-to, leave Jamie there while I visited the plant if it wasn't a school day. He loved the killer whales and dolphins. He loved the helicopter ride. He loved everything.

Today, after work, the idea was that I'd walk from the heliport to the Industrial Center Building, known as the ICB, where Stella had her studio, meet her there, and have supper at the Liberty Café across the street. It would only be a quarter of a mile longer than walking to the houseboat and it was a beautiful evening. Bikers, dog walkers, roller-bladers and runners passed me by as I strolled along the bike path at the waters edge. A bevy of coots paddled the water beside me, topsy-turvy ducks, velvety gray with white beaks, possessors of shrill quacks. I cut away from the water briefly at Gate Five Road, heading down to Clipper Yacht Harbor and Stella's studio.

The ICB was a gigantic Quonset hut, three stories high, and a block long. It was left over from World War II shipbuilding days when, in less than four years, Sausalito went from a coastal village to a major ship-building community. Marinship built fifteen Liberty ships, seventy-eight oil tankers, and twenty Army invasion barges. In the dread year of 1945, there were two American top-secret projects: the Manhattan Project in the desert ie: atomic bomb, and Dagwood in little old Sausalito.

If the atomic bomb didn't pan out, Dagwood was the alternative – a massive invasion of Japan, to which end barges were to be built and used to form breakwaters and unloading platforms for troops and weaponry. Each Dagwood was a floating concrete and steel caisson 230 feet long, 70 feet wide, and 60 deep. On the floor of the huge mold loft of the building, plans were drawn and the lines for the barges laid down. However, on August sixth the project was stopped cold because of the successful holo-caust of Hiroshima. "Bag Dagwood," said the Joint Chiefs, "the bomb is the way to go."

The building was now broken into a sixty room rabbit warren of stu-dios and offices, one of which Stella possessed. She was an independent woman. She wouldn't let me support her work and she paid for the studio and art materials from any paintings she was able to sell or from odd jobs she took on for her artist friends.

Now things were looking up for her. She was getting ready for a show in a Mill Valley gallery, the town next to Sausalito. Previously she had sold solely from her studio, mostly to friends. This would be her first show.

I climbed the stairs to the third floor. From the open studio door, I watched her. She stood poised in front of her easel with narrowed eyes, as if aiming the brush at the canvas. She reminded me of the long-beaked herons and egrets just before they unleashed the dart of their beaks for a fish. She was oblivious to my arrival and so I was able to view her in full creative mode. I felt proud of her intensity, her energy, how her whole mind and body fed through the brush to the canvas, and I appreciated why she was so tired after many hours in the studio.

She made a minuscule mark on the picture, her body relaxed, she sighed. Seeing me, she greeted me with a smile and a kiss. "Let me lock up here, and before we go to dinner I want to stop by a friend here in the building who is having a studio show. Is that okay?"

"Sure.'

She hung up her paint-splattered smock, preserved her brushes, turned off the light, and locked the door. She wore tan jeans, green cowboy boots, and a green suede shirt. (Stella did let me pay for her clothes.) She wore no makeup at all and it didn't matter. Her skin, eyes, brows, the line of her lips, couldn't be improved on in my eyes. Her only imperfection was crooked teeth which I found endearing.

"His name is Arnold," she said as we clattered down the stairs. "He paints eggs."

Arnold's studio was half the size of Stella's. It was crowded and, since people always surround Stella whenever she enters a room, I was able to instantly pocket the flamingo without being seen. It was on a windowsill with a plethora of other objects: clocks, postcards, family pictures, rocks, cups, trophies, and cactus plants. Luckily I was wearing a sport coat and the pockets were deep. The china figure was about five inches tall and almost that wide. I didn't get a good look at it, only saw the pink and snatched it without thinking, without even forming a decision. It was like an involuntary move, a hiccup.

But not that involuntary because I must have taken a sweeping look around first and, also, when I took it in my hand, I bent over to wipe something from my shoe as I slipped it into my pocket, a diverting action familiar to magicians and thieves. I'd always been good with my hands. But I'd never been devious until now or, rather, until my birthday night.

Joy had called me a few days after my birthday to say, "My 'mingo died."

I made the connection to the conversation we had had about Jamie. "You mean your little china animal is gone? You don't see it anymore?"

"Yes. It's gone, Uncle Tim, but I don't feel howible ..."

"That's all right because sometimes people and, er, things, die that we don't care enough about to feel sorry."

"It was a bad fwamingo."

"Oh, really? Why?"

"It wouldn't stand up."

"That is bad."

I'd noticed it was tottery. There was a chip off one foot, hence my finding it lying down in the dollhouse bathroom and now often recumbent on my bedside table. Unlike Joy, I forgave this behavior.

But back to Arnold's studio party; once the bird was in my pocket, my heart started to hammer away and the blood rushed to my face. My head throbbed. I felt it was making an audible throbbing noise, like an engine, or a pump, and I was sure I was breathing heavily, but no one seemed to notice any gasping or throbbing. No one looked at me funny.

I collected myself while feigning to look at the eggs. Then I really looked at the eggs. I went to the table and threw back a glass of howible wine. I identified Arnold as the man in the wheelchair, which made me go back and look at the trophies. He was a wheelchair marathoner. I strolled over and talked with him about marathons, telling him I'd run three before my knee broke down and that now I bike and kayak.

The eggs, which he blew the insides out of first, then painted, then framed, hanging them from metal strings in open boxes so they could be turned, were up on the walls, about twenty of them. They were intricate scenes of cars driving along roads, some in town, some in the country. He managed to pack a lot on the egg and achieve an amazing sense of space and dimension.

I knew Stella would like me to buy one, help Arnold along, but the fact was, the terrible secret was, I didn't like art. I didn't get it or care about it or want it or even see the point of it. Poor Stella. It was like a writer being married to an illiterate. She didn't know how deep my indifference went. Of course, I had always praised her pictures to the skies. Probably praise with no intelligence behind it doesn't go for much but she didn't complain. I'm a great believer in praise – for employees, wives, children, everyone. It's so easy and people thrive on it.

When we got to the Liberty Café, I went to the men's room and, once in the stall, took out the flamingo. It was pretty. The colors were soft and muted. His pink legs were set in brown and green grasses, on brown earth.

There was black on his wings and at the end of his beak. His eye was a black dot and, looking closely, I saw a bit of yellow around it. His breast was cream-colored and the rest of him, mainly the neck, back feathers, and legs, was pink. His wavy neck depended, head hanging down, unlike Joy's little one whose head looked upward. He looked forlorn, almost as if he might burst into tears. I put him in my briefcase, took a pee, washed up.

It occurred to me that, although Joy thought her flamingo was dead, it was really alive and well on my bedside table. Might not Jamie, too, be alive and well somewhere, not here on earth of course, but in some alternate universe, one that still had bikes and helicopters and dolphins?

Not a chance.

Stella was at the table. There was a candle and some tulips in a vase. "Hi, beautiful."

"Hi, handsome."

I wasn't handsome. At a distance I looked like I should be because I was tall, blond, well-built, with great teeth. But up close I clearly wasn't — my eyes were too small, my ears too big, and my hair was cut close around my ears so as to make them look even bigger because I couldn't stand to have people think I was trying to cover them with longer hair, like a man combing over a bald spot.

Stella said, "I was sort of hoping you would buy one of Arnold's eggs. It wouldn't take up much room and God knows you can afford it."

"Sorry." I did almost everything that she wanted except buy her friends' art.

She sighed. "Some day I'll find you an artist you like."

"I like you. You're my only artist. Next to you, everyone pales."

"Oh, really? Then I wonder why you didn't notice my new painting."

"?"

15

"On the easel in my studio."

I tried to envision it, but it was a blank. Gray, brown, and white probably, but otherwise …

"I guess I only had eyes for you." Which was true because of her intense pose, my seeing her not as my wife, but as a lone artist.

She didn't smile.

"We rushed away from your studio pretty quick."

Nowadays she got sullen along about her third drink. Sometimes it didn't take any drinks. "Have you ordered?"

"I could have in the time you were gone. I could have eaten."

It wasn't a great dinner.

That morning, before leaving for work, she had said, "Let's have dinner. I want to talk," and my heart leapt because I thought maybe, at last, she'd want to talk about Jamie and how she was feeling, because she had grown so impenetrable. And my greater hope, one that I hardly dared express even to myself, was that she'd talk about having another child, say she was ready. That was the birthday present I had hoped for the night we came home from George's.

But she didn't talk at all. She ate and drank and was quiet. When I tried various opening sentences, the most I could get out of her was a chewing sound.

"It wasn't a great dinner, James," I said before sleep. "Your mom was a pain in the ass." I had a little more latitude talking to Jamie now than when he was alive, but I'd always been open and frank with him. I'd been known to tell him about the great sex I had with his mom. I wanted him to know his mother was sexy and that sex was good to enjoy. He was thirteen when he died. I hope he'd had some sort of romance by then. I think he did. There was a girl he adored.

16

"Before dinner, I stole another flamingo, James. I stole it from a struggling artist, a cripple. How low can I get? What do you think of your old man now? You'd think I was a creep, right?" Creep was his worst word for someone. I smiled, feeling strangely pleased. "You'd be right, James."

"Tim?" Stella opened the guestroom door and peeked in. The Dagwood flamingo was still in my brief case but Uno, as I'd come to call the first flamingo, was in plain sight. I quickly grabbed him and said sternly, "I'm talking to Jamie."

"I know and I'm sorry to disturb your ritual, but I want to apologize for being such a bitch this evening." She entered the small room and sat on my bed, disturbing my ritual totally. She touched the hand that was hiding Uno. "You're making fists," she said, surprised. "Are you angry with me?"

I turned away from her, rolling to my side so I could drop my arm down the other side of the bed and toss Uno under it.

"Don't turn away from me," she said, not pleading, being firm. "I was upset this evening and the reason is ..."

I was suddenly terrified that she'd seen me steal Dagwood from her friend.

"I did something a few weeks ago, when you were away on business and I thought I could finally tell you about it, but then I realized that a restaurant would be the very worst place."

I felt extremely relieved it wasn't about Dagwood and then fell into a fit of anxiety about what it might be about. I sat up, bleating questions and she shushed me. Softly, she said, "I had my tubes tied."

"You didn't!"

"Yes. And it was more upsetting for me than I had expected. I came out of the anesthesia in tears. I'm all right now. I wanted to be completely all right before I told you ..."

17

"But, Stella," I interrupted. "How could you do this by yourself?"

"Oh, I didn't need you with me. It was simple and painless. They just go in through the belly button with an instrument and sort of solder them …"

"Stop! Stop! I can't stand it!"

"What?"

"I meant how could you have done this without consulting me? How could you take this decision by yourself? I can't believe you would do this to me."

"But, Tim, you knew I didn't want another child. We had talked about it a lot. Don't you remember?"

"I know we did, but it was right after. I thought for sure you'd change your mind. I thought after some time had passed we would both want another child. I've been waiting and hoping."

"You never mentioned it."

"I was waiting for you. I didn't want to pressure you."

"I told you I would never replace Jamie."

"It wouldn't be replacing …"

"See. We've gone over it and over it. The same old words every time."

We hadn't. We'd had one, maybe two conversations about it in the month after he died when she was open, when she was such a mess that she clung to me and talked and talked.

"Now the subject is closed forever," she said. "I waited a year to be sure and I am sure. I would be too scared to have another child. I wouldn't be able to paint, or do anything, except watch him constantly."

I began to feel furious. It was like the bereavement all over again — first disbelief, then grief, followed by anger. Acceptance was supposed to be the final stage. Good luck.

"You went behind my back, Stella."

"I honestly don't see it that way. It's a woman's prerogative. It's my body."

"It isn't. It isn't." The anger dissolved into heart-rending sadness. I started to cry, engulfed by tears and snot and choking sobs.

She threw her arms around me. "Don't, Tim. Oh, darling, please!"

It is even more painful when the person that has hurt you so much is also the only person who can comfort you.

III

FLOCK MATING

Although the next morning was Saturday, I was going into the office for a few hours because there was an ad campaign I'd put off looking at all week, knowing I was going to hate it. Stella was gone, probably to her studio. I hadn't gotten to sleep for hours after Stella disturbed my ritual with her ghastly news and then I slept badly. Howible dreams.

I took my cereal and strawberries out onto the deck and ate standing up, then put my bowl aside to turn on the hose. I watered my blimeys, a new kind of fruit. I had six planters full of them. This was the blimey deck. Stella got the other two decks for flowers.

In the lagoon, it was a minus tide, and about five egrets were browsing the shallow waters for nutrition, walking about with slow, studied steps, keenly eyeing the subsurface. I watched one dart his beak at a target with the speed of light, coming up with a nice little fish, probably an anchovy.

I surmised flamingoes were not unlike these egrets, having similar long legs and necks, only feathered pink instead of white, with thick, ungainly beaks rather than spears. The flamingo's beak was truly strange: burly and curved, a burden of a beak, it seemed to me, unlike any other bird's. I wondered why. I didn't really know anything about flamingoes except what I'd learned from looking at Uno and Dagwood, which reminded me to get poor Uno from under the bed and Dagwood out from my briefcase. And put them where? Where would Stella not find them and become deeply puzzled?

Jamie's house, of course! Perfect. I would go to Mill Valley after work, taking both Uno and Dagwood, and place them in our old unsold house. This decision made me feel unreasonably happy.

I watched the egrets, feeling honored to have them walking and grazing in my front yard, owning the place. The western sky reflected the sunrise to the east and the water carried on the reflection so the egrets and I were seeing more orange than blue. Then the hues dwindled away, returning water and sky to their accustomed shades of blue.

I took my dirty dish to the dishwasher then turned on my Web TV and roamed the internet for a flamingo web site.

These birds were five feet tall with a wingspan of five to six feet. They lived on volcanic mudflats and built foot-high nests out of the mud, living together by the thousands. They were pink from eating shrimp, a fact I accepted dubiously. Unlike the beak-darting egret, they swung their beaks back and forth in the water, sieving the small shrimps and algae.

They had large, fleshy tongues, which they used to push the water through the filaments and serrated edges of their beaks and they could draw the water into their bill and force it out again Twenty Times A Second! Impossible!

I tried moving my own tongue twenty times a second and I couldn't come close (only four times) and my tongue was not large and fleshy. It was comparatively streamlined. This had to be a misprint, a cyber-miss, or else they, the cyber-people, took me for a gullible idiot.

Mating only occurs in large flocks, or *mats*. Elaborate breeding displays, such as head flagging, wing saluting, and twist preening, precede mating. I could sort of visualize the second two but was bewildered by the first. Still, it all sounded cool. Some bird.

I bicycled to the Zeus offices in San Rafael, taking the bike path and back roads so that a ten-minute car drive became the journey of an hour. Funny to one day take a helicopter to save an hour's drive and the next day take a bicycle to add an hour's commute. Such was the life of Tim.

I thought I was going to spend a half day at the office with the ad campaign material but it was worse than anticipated so it was seven o'clock when I got to the Mill Valley house, Jamie's house, where he had spent his thirteen years. I had stopped to get an order from MacDonald's on the way, something I hadn't done since Jamie was alive when we would get gigantic orders together, although he, being a vegetarian, would order a Big Mac, hold the burger, or an egg McMuffin, fries and onion rings.

The house waited: pale yellow on a green lawn. One rambling story built circa 1900, when some whimsical builder wanted to see how many French doors and many-paned windows he could fit in and still have wood left over to hang them from. There was a six-pack in the fridge so I cracked a beer and sat on the porch glider that Goodwill was supposed to take when we moved but had refused on the grounds it was too beat up even for them. Good thing. I loved that glider and there was no place else to sit.

A gardener came fairly regularly to keep things looking nice for the rest of the neighborhood and the front garden gleamed in the evening sun. I put Dagwood and Uno on the porch railing then ate my meal, missing my son.

It was near nine o'clock and I was into my fourth beer when George showed up carrying a six-pack. "Stella didn't know where you were so I figured you for here." He put on the porch light, sat down beside me, and opened a beer for both of us. "Don't glide, okay?"

His kindly face looked tired so I hastened to unburden myself before he began telling me how tired he was which he loved to do. Like many people with incredible energy, he expended it to the last drop and naturally was tired before he recharged, but it never occurred to him that his fatigue was natural. He worried about being tired. I had half his energy but only spent half of my half each day and so was never tired.

I told him about Stella's self-imposed operation. "I felt so bad, George. It was like Jamie dying all over again. On top of that, it was such a betrayal, her doing it behind my back like that, then just telling me as if it were nothing, nothing for me, and only a little unsettling for her. For me, the thought of our never having another child, just being the two of us for-ever, with her painting, my juice, is deeply depressing. Life is so empty, George – if it's possible to be empty and unbearable at the same time. The fact is they say you get over a child's death, but you don't. I'm never going to get over it and now, there's nothing even to hope for."

I went on like that. It all poured out. I opened two more beers. I un-burdened myself almost word for word two or three times more. "I know I have a lot to be thankful for: my own great business, piles of money, a beautiful, talented wife whom I love and who I think loves me, some of the time. I've got my health. I've got you, Laurie, and Joy. I tell myself ten times a day how lucky I am and it doesn't do any fucking good."

Then George, who had been listening quietly the whole time, about an hour, said the strangest thing, something I would never have expected in a thousand years. He said, "Would you like to go to an orgy?"

I choked on my beer, spraying it over both of us. "An orgy? Are you kidding? You mean ... an orgy?"

"Yeah, Ears, an orgy. He called me Ears when we were alone, always had.

"Is this a regular thing with you?"

"No. Maybe once a month. It does me good. It's like getting totally drunk. Cleans out the system. A tune-up."

"Does Laurie know?"

23

"Not really."

What was 'not really' supposed to mean? Either you really knew your husband went to orgies or you really didn't. I decided not to pursue it. It was enough to entertain this new and outlandish view of my doctor brother. Still, my pecker was coming alive. Weird. I would never go to an orgy. I would never even think about it.

"So, do you want to come? It's here in Mill Valley. Not far. Nice people."

"Men and women?"

"Of course men and women. It takes two to tango."

"I mean, is the sex between either or what?"

"This is a heterosexual orgy, but there are homosexual ones, or bi."

"Here in Mill Valley? I can't believe this."

I was feeling totally hot.

"Come on. We'll take my car. Put your bike on the rack so I can drive you home after." Before he turned off the porch light, he picked up Dagwood from the railing and said, "Pretty."

"Dagwood," I introduced. "And the other one is Uno."

"Right. Glad you're fixing up the place."

It was a big house in one of the canyons, set back from the road but not too far back, and not that far from the houses on either side. I wondered about any carrying coitus calls ringing through the neighborhood. Maybe the orgy house was sound proof.

"What about condoms?" I asked as we got out of the car.

"They're all over the place. There's no liquor, although it's okay to drink before you arrive, like we did. They don't let anyone in who is drunk or obstreperous."

I was feeling nervous now but my pecker was hard as a rock. "So, what do we do?"

"Just come with me to the door."

"And say Joe sent me?"

"Sort of. There's a password. It's a club, really."

An orgy club. My pecker felt like a club.

"We'll go right to one of the bathrooms, undress, comb our hair, if we have any. Follow me."

At the door, words were spoken to the doorman, money passed hands. I followed George down the hall into the bathroom. We hadn't been naked together since we were kids, teenagers. Then he'd gone off to college and med school and I lost him for about ten years. He was three years older than me. Our dad died young and George looked out for me all through grade school and middle school. Nobody got to bully me or call me Dumbo because of my ears.

His body was shorter than mine, more powerful, hairier. By now my nerves had lost my boner and I could see that our cocks were similar. His testicles were bigger. We took quick showers and dried off. I wanted him to throw his arm around me the way he did when he was drunk but he didn't, so I put my arm around him. I could feel the side of his body against mine and it was nice. "Thanks," I said, meaning thanks for trying to cheer me up in this totally bizarre way.

"You lucky bastard," he said. "You can go out there without holding your stomach in."

People stood around talking, sipping pure mountain spring water and Zeus Juice. Some were dancing. Some were out on the deck, leaning on the railing, or swilling around in the Jacuzzi. Everyone was naked. I felt at a loss not being able to judge anyone by their clothing, which was important to me. I like to be able to stereotype. The light was mellow but not dim. There was conversation and laughter. All in all I think it was a subdued orgy as orgies go. I followed George around like a little brother. Several of the women greeted him happily. None of the women were dogs, although they were nowhere near in Stella's category. Still, some of them were lovely, one or two. I shouldn't even be thinking of Stella.

George went off with two women. I started to follow him but another woman intercepted me. "Let's dance," she said.

I looked yearningly after George. Then I looked at her. She was thin with small breasts that had incredibly rosy nipples. I peered at them, wondering if they had been doctored. Stella's nipples were brown – but I wasn't going to think about Stella.

Despite the mating occurring in large flocks, no elaborate breeding displays were being exhibited. Humans are so constrained in these matters, so unimaginative compared to birds. I did a little head flagging, although not too clear exactly what that move entailed, and limited by my comparatively short neck. I wasn't even going to think about twist preening. It would be hopeless without feathers.

George was disappearing down the hall into, I presumed, a bedroom. I felt abandoned. I couldn't stop thinking about Stella, my darling, the love of my life, to whom I'd never been unfaithful. I'd slept with two women before I met Stella at age eighteen and never looked back. What was I doing here?

I began backing out of the room. I had a sensation of fading into the woodwork, something I'd always wanted to do. However, it was essential to fade into the woodwork where my clothes were. I found them, donned them, and crept away into the night. I got my bike from George's car, mounted it, and wobbled away down the canyon until, braced by the night air, I began to peddle properly. I biked through the town, to the outskirts, to the bike path where it was clear sailing to Sausalito and our floating home.

I felt better. My head was empty. The sad thoughts would come thronging back, but for now, pedaling ever faster along the water's edge under a lopsided moon, I experienced a time of grace.

At the houseboat, I poked my head into Stella's bedroom. "I'm home."

"Were you with George?" she asked sleepily.

"Yes."

"That's good. He wanted to talk to you. 'Night."

I laid out my clothes for the next day: white tee shirt since it was Sunday, khaki shorts, Indian bead belt Jamie gave me, topsiders, no sweater. It was going to be warm. I put today's clothes in the washer and laundry bag. I talked to James but did not tell him about the orgy. I fell asleep between the I love you and the goodnight.

"Tim?"

"Huh?"

"There's this noise."

I was being shaken into minor alertness. The woman, my wife, didn't understand that I hadn't slept at all the night before, thanks to her, and today had bicycled forty miles, all told, exhausted myself working until seven, then had drunk beer by myself, then more beer while whining to George. The day had ended with me fading into the woodwork, which was extremely difficult and tiring as it means changing the molecules of the entire body, and that was followed by more bicycling.

"Listen!" she demanded.

I loaned her my big ears. I was willing to do that as long as I didn't have to get up. I heard some kind of motor sound. "Dishwasher," I concluded, closing my eyes and ears.

The body shaking began again. "The dishwasher is not on and this is not a fridge sound or furnace. Nothing is on."

Stella was unduly sensitive to sounds in general, however small, but this was, I had to admit, a hell of a loud sound. When we had first moved onto the boat, it was connected to one of the pilings by a steel collar and the collar squeaked and howled when the boat was moving, a sound I kind of liked, but Stella was made insomniac and had me replace it with ropes. It was a peaceful place to live. No highway sound, quiet neighbors. When it was windy, it shrieked around the house, maybe because there were no trees to impede it, but at the same time one didn't have to worry about branches falling on the roof as we had in Jamie's house. Now, here was this machine sound vibrating through our abode as if we were in the factory district of a major city.

As long as she knew what the noise was and that it was uncontrollable, like the wind, say, she could resign herself. My job now was to name the noise.

"Tim, I've been all over the house, but it seems equally loud everywhere downstairs, a little quieter upstairs. Please get up and see."

I listened. It seemed to have a throb. Like a pump.

"I think it's a pump. Maybe the neighbors have a leak. I'll ask tomorrow."

"What's queer is that when I go outside, I can't hear it. It's definitely here in the house."

She was working herself up now. She was going to cry.

"There," I said. "It stopped." I felt proud, as if my listening to it had stopped it. Then it started again. Shit.

"It started again," she said needlessly. She sat on my bed, collapsed into a heap of misery. She wept. To me, it didn't seem worth crying about compared to what I'd cried about the night before, no more children ever, but that's how life is. She pulled off my covers. "Come."

"Come and do what?"

"Come and listen."

"I'm listening. I hear it. You said it's the same all over the house so why should I get up? I'm sure it's nothing dangerous. It's just a neighbor's really loud pump. I'll talk to them tomorrow. I can't call them at," I eyed the clock, "three a.m."

"But you're going back to sleep and I'm not."

"Right," I said, and I did.

We slept late and when I woke up she was in my arms, having slept the rest of the night with her husband, the man she had so blithely double-crossed. Without telling me, she had gone and sealed her body off forever from my sperms. Our lovemaking would never again be the creative act it was meant to be and yet she seemed to have no grasp of the enormity of her deed. She had lain in my arms as if it were a night like any other of the seven thousand three hundred nights of our marriage.

IV

FISH STORY

"What are you going to do today?" Stella asked me during breakfast after I'd watered the blimeys, some of which were beginning to fruit, one of which was ready to eat. We shared it out. It tasted like a combination of lime and melon, which it was, a curious new fruit conceived by a fellow dockster. It was a tasty shower of juice in the mouth.

"Tim?"

"Do? Nothing. Read the paper. Maybe take the kayak out. You?"

"I'm going to the studio." She finished her coffee and stood up, grabbing her purse from which she extracted a lipstick and small mirror. This one lipstick was her only make-up and only sometimes – I could never tell which times and why those times. The mirror, which she'd had forever, featured a picture of Christo's running Fence, an installation the artist created thirty miles to the north of us which Stella had worked on.

"Which reminds me," she said, smacking her reddened lips, "Somebody stole Arnold's flamingo at his studio party. Can you believe it?"

With a qualm, I remembered I'd left Dagwood on the porch railing of Jamie's house. I doubted Stella ever drove by. Probably never. And if she did, she wouldn't see the flamingo from the road. But I'd better bring it in. I could kayak to Bay Front Park in Mill Valley and walk to the house from there. It would make a good outing. I loved to exercise with a destination in mind, some chore to do, like the terrible chore of heading for a certain café for a cup of coffee.

"Tim?"

"I assume you don't mean an actual bird was stolen."

"No, a china one. Very tacky. Who would want one enough to steal it?"

I felt indignant that Stella thought Dagwood was tacky, and also frustrated that I couldn't get into an argument with her about it. Dagwood was the prettiest china ornament I'd ever seen, not that I'd ever been an ornament aficionado. I'm an athlete and a businessman. Until Joy, I never went in for that sissy sort of thing. Alpha male. Tough guy.

I wanted to tell Stella that my Dagwood was so much more beautiful and artistic than Arnold's eggs that it wasn't funny. Dagwood could eat his eggs for breakfast. Sieve them through his bill twenty times a second. Okay, fifteen. Nine.

Had she ever even looked at Dagwood? She probably just had some generic idea of china flamingoes. "Tacky?" I asked calmly.

"Garish, gaudy, tasteless, tawdry."

This did not at all describe Dagwood with his subtle colors, elegant pose, and sorrowful demeanor.

"Carnival fare," she continued her barrage of insults. "Low class. Something someone would collect who knew nothing about art."

"Collect?" My ears pricked. With my ears this was a sight to see, photo op.

"Oh, yes. They go back to the fifties and there are avid flamingo collectors. Arnold said people had offered to buy it from him."

"How much did they offer?"

"Oh, I don't know. Twenty bucks. Fifty."

I was relieved, which made me realize I didn't want to have stolen something valuable because then it would look like serious thieving instead of what it was, which I didn't know what that was, but it wasn't about greed or gain or collecting. It seemed to be something about feeling better. In the pink.

"Anyhow, I feel sorry for Arnold because it was his mother's. Excuse me, I've got to pee." She ran downstairs.

Great. Now I'd stolen the crippled, struggling-artist's, dead-mother's flamingo. This theft looked worse and worse. Creeping creepism. But I could always give it back. What prevented me from giving it back whenever I wanted to give it back? Right now, I didn't want to, but maybe someday I would. Looked at in that light, I'd only borrowed it.

Stella returned, kissed me, as she always did when greeting or parting, a brief pressure of the lips, a fluttering wing of hair against my cheek, the singular scent of her, the lipstick taste. "Don't forget we're going to the Steins tonight. Seven o'clock."

"Who are the Steins?"

"The couple we met at George and Laurie's on your birthday. They live here in Sausalito. See you around six."

"But, wait, if we're going to see George tonight, why was he looking for me last night?"

"There was something he wanted to talk to you about privately."

I checked the tides on my tidal calendar and paddled to Mill Valley in the early afternoon. The ocean-going kayak skimmed the surface of the water like a bird or fish, both of which the fairly healthy bay was full. Flocks of gulls, terns, and shorebirds filled the water and air with the occasional super-winged heron or egret. It was like being in a National Geographic special. One flock of little sandpiperish birds, about fifty of them, flying as one organism, like bees, lifted into the air, synchronized, turned their bodies one way, and in an act of color camouflage, faded into the skywork, disappeared, then wheeled, and reappeared.

I even saw a stingray swimming by, its huge triangular shape leaving an odd wake, its rubbery, bat-wing flippers tipping up into the air with each stroke.

I paddled by the last of the outlaw anchor-outs, houseboats that by law should be tied to the dock, but were stubbornly anchored out in the bay, weird constructions of wood, tar paper, and glass that formed superstructures on wooden hulls, some surrounded by floats with piles of junk. These folks lived off the grid. Each anchor-out had a dory to row back and forth for supplies and, hopefully, to aid in properly disposing of his waste, often with a dog standing in the bow as George Washington is seen to do in pictures. They all seemed to have a resident dog. The authorities were unable to force these folks off the bay. They had to wait for the eventual sinking of the craft, which, by the look of some of them, would be soon.

I left the kayak at Mill Valley's Bay Front Park dock, hoping it wouldn't be stolen, and hoofed it to Jamie's house. I put the two flamingoes indoors, grabbed a nap on the glider before heading back. Despite checking the tides before I left, the nap delayed me, and I had to battle my way against the current and against a twenty-knot wind. It had been the windiest spring and summer in history. Some of the tossed air was down from Alaska with a non-California bite to it.

I was wrung-out when I clambered onto our float and Stella was mad at me for being late. She stomped around, flailed her arms, and berated me. Even when I showered, she shouted at me over the water sound — no stripping down and jumping in with me to have sudden sex like the old days. I tried to think if she had been mad at me so much when Jamie was alive. I think not. I think she worked too hard at her painting now and was over-stressed — maybe because of the show coming up. More likely it was that, with the loss of my boy, I had become a maddening person. That was probably it.

George and Laurie were at the Steins' dinner party, just the six of us. It turned out Marie Stein was a psychiatrist. She was pretty, stylish, about my age only, unlike me, had matured. Her serious eyes were dark blue beneath her straight, serious brows, contrasting with fluffy auburn hair. We stood on the deck of their hillside home and looked at San Francisco, a white geometric jumble between the blue bay and sky. She asked me about the death.

"The car was full of eighth-graders. It was one of the kids' birthdays. The older brother, a teenager, was driving. Jamie didn't have a belt on. There were no belts left because the car was jammed full. The driver burned rubber out of the driveway and the door popped open, or wasn't properly closed to begin with, and Jamie fell out. They took him to emergency. We met him there. He was okay. No bones broken. No concussion, just a really bad bruise on his thigh, which developed a blood clot. Some hours later, this clot went to his heart and stopped it. We found him dead in his bed the next morning."

Marie was quiet, then asked, "How are you doing, Tim?"

"Not too well. Stella and I had grief counseling for about six months. We moved to a new house. But ..."

Again she waited a beat. "The worst thing that can happen to a person," she said, "is to lose a child. It's out of the natural order of things. It will take a long time for you to recover."

"Thank you. Those words are music to my ears. You can't imagine how many people think I should be okay by now."

"You may never get over it," she said.

"Oh, thank you!" I hugged her almost passionately. I was so grateful. She understood. She knew.

"I gather you are not a religious person. It's too bad. Faith is an incredible healer."

"Are you religious, Marie?"

"Yes, I am."

Alvin came out, carrying a platter of meat and looked at me sternly as if I shouldn't be talking with his wife without paying her. "Ah" he said, "the coals look just right," then he proceeded to burn the hell out of our steaks. Why do men who can't cook in a pan think they can cook on a grill? However, the salad Stella brought was perfect and Alvin only half-incinerated the corn.

After dinner, I followed Marie into her kitchen while she made the coffee. Whammo! Two flamingoes sat on the breadbox — extremely pink. They were a sugar bowl and cream pitcher. One flamingo's neck formed the handle of the creamer. For the sugar bowl, the upper half of the body was the cover. They were delightful. They lit up the kitchen. She didn't put them on the tray with the coffee since they were too small to serve the six of us.

My heart started to beat, my mind to buzz. Now I was going to steal from my hostess, the woman who had been kind to me, who had understood that I would never recover from Jamie. This would be a new low. Arnold, at least, although crippled and struggling, and orphaned, hadn't been kind to me.

But I couldn't do it tonight because it would obviously point to me as the thief. I would have to come back for them sometime when the Steins weren't home. I would have to break into their house and rob it. My heart sang.

As we left the party I asked George what he wanted to talk to me about. He said to get together with him later in the week.

That night, Stella woke me again. Third night in a row. Grounds for divorce. She turned on my lamp and sat on my bed.

"Look, Stella," I grumbled. "I've got work in the morning. You can sleep as late as you want."

"I have work, too," she flashed back at me. "My painting is work. It is not a hobby. I go to the studio every day. My show is in a month."

In truth, Stella worked much harder than I did. This past year I'd hardly worked at all, only went through the motions, sometimes not even that. I'd leave for work but end up somewhere else – a movie, a hike on Mt. Tamalpais, a long drive. "All right, all right, what's the problem tonight?"

"It's the noise," she said. "It's back. Did you speak to the neighbors?"

"No, I didn't. Because it was gone this morning and I forgot about it. As did you," I added pointedly.

I listened. Tonight it sounded like an airplane off in the distance, the near distance – only the sound of the near-distant airplane definitely came from our houseboat.

"Please do something. It's driving me mad."

"It's one a.m. What should I do?"

"Call Julio."

He was our neighbor to the left. I fought with her about waking Julio, but she was in an irrational state and I gave in. The difference between a woman and a terrorist is that you can negotiate with a terrorist. I called Julio. I told him about the noise, asked him if he had a pump going, or a generator, or was in possession of a subterranean firing range.

36

He answered at length and I began to laugh. I was still laughing when I hung up. "Stella, my love, it is the Humming Toadfish, also called Singing Fish or Plainfin Midshipman. Doing his mating call. It has a gas bladder like a frog that makes a noise that, as it echoes and vibrates off the hull of the boat, gets really loud. They lay their eggs on or under the hull, whereupon the male hums, buzzes, and groans to protect them. They just sing at night. During the day they bury themselves in the mud, something I might start doing myself. They like new hulls, like ours, because there are no barnacles or mussels attached. Cheer up. They'll be gone in a month or two."

"Unbelievable," she shook her head. "Fish."

"Apparently, in the dock lease we signed, we promised to understand about the Humming Toadfish."

I turned over, facing the wall, "Goodnight, Stella by Starlight. Sweet dreams. I love you." I said I love you automatically but did I still love her? Yes. I did. I always would. I mated for life. I shut my eyes. "Get the light on your way out."

She remained sitting on the bed. "What were you talking about with Marie when you were alone on the deck with her, hugging her?"

"Jamie. I told her about his death. She said I'd never get over it."

"That's a horrible thing to say."

"Howible, but twu, Stella."

"I hate it when you talk like Joy. You're just masking your feelings by being cute."

Right. But what's wrong with cute? What's wrong with anything that helps?

Eyes open, I turned onto my back and looked at her. I decided to speak from the heart, something I was getting out of the way of doing, being a

37

quip-master instead. "Your feelings are so masked you never mention him. You won't listen to me talk to Jamie before bed and you won't talk about him with me or with anyone. You never mention his name. Stella, we are the only two people in the world who remember every single thing about him. We could reminisce. I need that from you. Desperately. So we'll never forget all the little things ..." I was choking up, but determined not to cry. "Please, don't forsake me."

She hung her head. Her beautiful hair slipped over her lovely face. "You are right, Tim. Thank you for saying that. From now on, make me talk about Jamie. Pry it out of me."

We reached for each other.

V

FLAMINGO BURGLARY

The following Thursday, on my way to see George for our mysterious talk, I bought a Porsche, the new Boxster. I'd been driving my old Saab around for years and felt the need of a change. Still, it was a sudden decision.

They'd sold out the 1999 and the 2000 Boxster wasn't in until the New Year, but one customer had a change of heart so the dealer said it was mine. The little roadster was pale yellow. I'd have liked faded-Levi blue, but they didn't make such a color and, although white was good for shirts, it wasn't for cars and I deplored the ubiquitous silver. I couldn't get any kind of deal on this their only car, so I wrote a check for sixty thousand and drove away.

George's house was in the opposite canyon of the orgy house. Mill Valley has two canyons, with a ridge in between. They both have creeks running through from the mountain's springs and run-off. Mt. Tamalpais constitutes the backdrop of the town, a twenty-five hundred foot rise above the valley, home of the giant redwoods, Sequoia Sempervirens. Many of the huge trees were clustered around George's house and even in July you could hear the creek going by. Joy and I could hear it because we were in it, trying to catch crayfish, not succeeding, but having fun getting wet and muddy. I pretended to slip, and fell on my ass in the water. Joy was weak with laughter while I acted outraged and upset, flailing around, trying to regain my feet, falling down again. "Oww!" I cried, "My bottom! I hurt my bottom!"

Joy reeled with laughter, finally falling on her own little butt. After a while, seeing she was beginning to shiver from the wet and from being in the shade of the trees, I carried her piggyback to the house. We went inside and built a fire, changing our clothes in front of it, after raiding the closet for a pair of George's jeans, all too big. I found cargo pants, which weren't, and Joy found a tee shirt of his that was red.

"I can't wear red."

"What's wong with wed?"

"Haven't you noticed I always wear white shirts?

"Why, Uncle Tim?"

"Because I have to. Big trouble would come if I didn't. But wearing George's red shirt doesn't count because he's my brother."

"But why only white?"

"I'm compulsive. Maybe, if you are lucky, you, too, can be compulsive when you grow up. That means you feel you have to do things that aren't really important, but seem terribly important. Like, I always have to be on time places, unlike your Dad."

"I heard that," said George, coming in. He picked up Joy and gave her a kiss.

"We fell down in the cweek," she said happily.

"Good for you."

After George had changed out of his doctor's garb and rejoined us, Joy went off for supper with her nanny.

"Man, am I tired, "George began. "Open heart surgery today ..."

Before he began to execute a long plaint, I said, "Beautiful new nanny. Scandinavian?"

George looked surprised, as if he hadn't noticed. "Nanny? No, she's from around here, just graduated from Cal., helping us out in exchange for room and board while she looks for work."

Having brushed the beautiful nanny aside, he told me how tired he was and I commiserated. Then, looking serious, he told me he had to sell his stock in Zeus Juice. I owned forty-five percent and he owned ten. Five other guys shared the rest.

"I have to do it. Laurie was going to return to work when Joy was one, then when she was two. Now, Joy's three and it's clear Laurie is not going back to the law. Which is fine with me. However, she made more money than I did. Suddenly I've got college to pay for my other two." He referred to his daughters from his first marriage both of whom lived on the east coast. "And I'm thinking of cutting back on my own practice. To study."

"You don't have to explain. I understand."

"I hate to do it. Can you buy the stocks from me? Enough to keep a controlling interest?"

"No. I haven't the cash."

"You could if you sold Jamie's house."

I laughed. "You don't understand. We're talking millions here."

"We are?"

"But don't worry. I'll still be the major stockholder."

"If you just purchased enough to have fifty one percent, you'd be safe."

"Can't do it. Even if I hadn't just bought a Porsche."

His face lit up. He stopped looking tired and concerned. "Is that your Boxster out there?"

"Yes. Do you remember that Dad had a Porsche Boxer? He was the only man in Maine in the fifties who had a foreign sports car. The Boxster was sort-of named after that model."

"Cool. Was that the one he drove into the tree?"

"No, but that was a foreign car, too."

"Let's take a whirl, man. What are we sitting here for?"

"Okay, but find me a white shirt, first, to put over this garish tee."

We snaked over the mountain road to Stinson Beach and had dinner together at the Sand Dollar, linguine with mussels and tomato sauce. We almost always ate the same thing at restaurants. After our Mud Pie dessert, (a chocolate-covered, ice cream and cookie concoction, which originated at that restaurant, so they bragged) George said he had to be getting back. "Tonight is my flogging night," he said.

"Come on, tell me this isn't true. You're joking."

George was a consummate joker and I would normally assume he was putting me on if it hadn't been for the orgy night.

"Not joking."

"S&M?"

"We at the flogging club like to call it flogging."

"Oh, man!" I put my head in my hands. "Are you the flogger or the floggee?"

"Flogger of course." He puffed out his chest and smiled.

This was beyond the pale. "George, please tell me you wouldn't hit a woman."

"Of course not, only the ones who want to be hit."

"I see."

"Rest assured I don't use my bare hands. Whips and cat-o'-nine-tails. Sledgehammers. Stuff like that. I wear a belt with spikes on it," he said happily. "And sort of a Viking helmet. With horns."

"And a bear-fur breechclout no doubt."

"Exactly. With the claws on. Very sexy. I'm not going to invite you along this time. Sorry."

"Now I feel hurt. But, I can't come anyhow, I have nothing to wear."

"White shirts need not apply," he said.

After a return drive with the sun going down behind the Pacific and the stars splattering the sky as if thrown by a giant hand, the car handling like an angel, I dropped George at his house and hoped he'd stay there.

A few nights later, the Steins were coming to the houseboat for a barbecue with George, Laurie, and some of our new dock friends. I had told Stella I'd be late home.

I parked on the main drag of Sausalito, Bridgeway, waited for the Steins to go by in their green BMW and ducked when they did. Then I drove up to their house and parked a block away. Before I'd left their house a week ago, I'd released the latch on their bathroom window. If it had since been re-locked, I'd have to break the pane. First I rang the doorbell to be sure no one was home. No answer. Originally I'd thought to make a real burglary of it, take a lot of stuff, making the flamingoes seem incidental, but I bagged that idea for a raft of reasons, deciding I'd just swipe the birds and the Steins could wonder about their oddball disappearance until their dying days.

The bathroom window was actually open a bit and when I stuck my head in, I could smell why. Surely this was Alvin's doing. Marie would never leave a stink. I wriggled through, hands and head first, landing on my hands, then walking them along to let in the rest of my body.

I opened the bathroom door quietly and stepped out. Something hit me hard in the legs and I fell with a crash. One of my shoes flew off. It was a bulldog! Where had he come from? No dog the other night when we were here. But I could see why they might want to contain him when guests arrived.

My heart was thudding. The dog was coughing and snorting instead of barking. Maybe it was his idea of a growl. The sweat stood out on my

43

brow but, rather than re-attacking the downed invader (me), he went after my topsider, crunching it between his jaws and shaking his head as if he were subduing a small animal, all the while breathing hard through his receding nose.

I laughed, realizing he was a puppy, playing. He was white with some tan patches here and there. "Here, boy." He bowlegged it over to me and jumped on my lap, licking my face. His tongue was about a yard long. Really wet. He had a mouth like a Right Whale, halfway up his head. His muscular body was as wide as it was high.

But time was scurrying by. I got up from the floor and went to the kitchen. The puppy followed me, making a grab for my pants legs, his nails clicking on the tiles. I was wearing George's cargo pants and I put the two flamingoes in the voluminous pockets. I also wore a baseball cap, frontward, George's unreturned red tee shirt, rubber gloves. This embarrassing outfit was my burglar disguise. While I was standing still, Bullpuppy got a good bite on my pant leg and with his impassioned head shaking back and forth made a tear, ripping it up to my calf. The dog was going to be good at his job once he stopped being adorable.

I played with him a little longer. I was in love. If the Steins weren't at my houseboat, I'd have taken him home. I'd change from being a flamingo thief to a puppy thief. Why hadn't I bought a dog instead of a car? But who would take care of him during the day? It wouldn't be fair. Well, who took care of this puppy? Probably they had a dog walker but walkers didn't roll around on the floor and play, nor I'm sure, did the Steins.

With a farewell kiss, I let myself out the front door. At the car, I changed back into my jeans and white button-down shirt, wrapping the birds in the other clothes, and leaving them in the trunk. Then, with a mighty Porschean roar, I headed for home boat.

When I sauntered in, and greeted everyone, Stella asked, "What on earth happened to your shoe?" and I could swear that in Marie Stein's puzzled glance at my mangled shoe was the recognition of the distinctive look of Bullpuppy's work. Before leaving I should have checked his teeth for cargo pant threads.

Stella had started the barbecue. I got the chicken breasts I'd been marinating to the deck where I found Alvin, the terrorist griller, had taken a stance, prepared to dictate to me regarding the coals' readiness on my own home deck. "Just in time," he said approvingly.

"Almost," I said, with an air of quiet authority. Then I told him rather gushingly about my blimeys, just to annoy him, and cause him anxiety, by delaying the grilling. He paid no attention to my fruitistic enthusiasm and interrupted to say that the coals were now beyond ready and rapidly losing heat. His controllingness, something his psychiatrist wife should deal with, made me tarry almost too long, but the chicken came out just fine, perhaps not as crispy as I might have liked.

It was a good party and Stella and I both slept through the night together to the tune of the humming Toadfish.

VI

FLAMINGO UGLY

I regret stealing the ugly flamingo, a blight upon the collection — no, not the collection, the flock or, more properly, the *mat*. I hadn't found a flamingo to steal for over a week and I abducted it because I was out of control. I'd taken to looking through antique shops, having exhausted, it seemed to me, the possibility of stealing from family and friends and struggling artists and yes, my own employees, one of whom I'd discovered had a flamingo coffee mug, which I came in to work on a weekend day to disembarrass her of, and yes, from the Catholic Church. I'd stolen from God Himself. In the church's rummage shop, I had found a flamingo spoon-holder, the kind you set a cooking utensil on, that you've stirred something with, so that you don't dirty the counter – although I personally think it's easier to wipe a counter than wash a spoon-holder, especially one with engraved feathers.

So far, at Jamie's house, the *mat* consisted of Uno, Dagwood, the Steins' sugar and creamer, the mug, and the spoon-holder. Each one stood for a little heart-stopping adventure. Funny that it was when my heart stopped that I felt most alive.

I had taken the day off work, as I was doing most days these days, to take Joy to the beach. The nanny came, too, holding Joy on her lap in the Boxster, but she left us alone to stroll the beach and see how many men would stroll after her, falling in line almost militaristically. She accumulated seven. Men and boys stopped playing Frisbee and football, stopped boogie-boarding and wave-surfing, just to fall in behind her and be a for-lorn retinue. It was a sad commentary on my sex.

"Try not to be too beautiful when you grow up," I told Joy.

"I alweddy am beautiful," she said and then, with that wonderful change-of-subject ability kids have, "Marie has a bull god."

"Marie Stein?"

"Yes, a white bull god. Flintstone. I love him."

"I've seen that dog. I love him, too."

"I want a puppy so bad."

"What do your folks say?"

"I have to be old-nuff to take care of him. But I *am* old-nuff."

"Dogs can be a lot of work, honey. I guess you have to be old enough to take him for a walk three or four times a day. When I was little, dogs could run around town, but now there is a leash law.'

"Me no like dat leash law."

"Try to say *I* don't like that leash law."

"*I* no like dat leash law."

"I don't either. I tell you what. We'll ask Marie if we can borrow Flintstone during the day. I bet she'll be glad to lend him to us so he can play. Now let's go for a swim."

We went into the frigid, northern California waters, Joy on my shoulders. The water was unswimmable most years except for maybe two weeks in late August and this year it was five degrees colder than its usual fifty-eight because of La Nina, the same weather condition that had brought the Alaskan wind. The icy water was just another way of stopping my heart to feel alive. You'd think the nanny would have done it for the day, but she didn't. Funny about that. She left me cold, just as she apparently did George. The icy water also allowed me to scream along with Joy, something men rarely get to do. We played in the waves, Joy on my back, arms around my neck, as I rode the rollers to the sand, and we soon forgot the cold in the fun of it all.

After the swim, I left Nanny and Joy on the beach and moseyed into the village. I climbed a flight of stairs that switch-backed upward into Jack's Alleged Antiques, perched on the second floor of a tottery building above a small cheerful plant nursery.

I wasn't in my burglar's disguise but I did have on dark glasses, baseball cap, and bathing suit, with a white short-sleeved shirt, unbuttoned to show my manly chest. The rest was skin, fairly sunburned. I looked like a million guys. The cap detracted from my ears since the bill stuck out more than they did, just barely.

I thought it was too bad for this terrific little village to host such a deplorable store. I hate stores like this that look bad and smell bad. I felt loath to touch anything for fear I'd get hepatitis. There were old postcards, tools, bottles, paperbacks, doodads, knick-knacks, utensils, dishes, vases, pictures, bowls, broken furniture and one pink flamingo.

In a flash, I stuck it under my shirt and pressed it to my side with my elbow. I angled back toward the entrance.

The guy presiding over this dismal shop, presumably Jack himself, wore muttonchops, imagining he was living in the time of Dickens, they being a beard which flowed from the sideburns, covering just the part of the jaw that clenches, but not the chin or upper lip.

He looked like a fool but he wasn't one. "What have you got there, buddy?"

I could do one of several things: run like hell, holding the pink flamingo like a curly pink baton to be passed to the next runner, or cravenly pay for it, or set it on the counter and say I was thinking about it, then go look at other stuff until he was distracted by another customer, if he ever got other customers, at which time I'd abscond with it. But, if I did that, he might put it aside on the shelf behind him instead of leaving it on the counter. I knew I wasn't going to pay for it. Flamingo thieves don't pay.

"Atchoo!" I sneezed into both hands making it look like I'd tucked the flamingo away to do just that. It was a legitimate sneeze since I had the dust of the ages up my nose, Jack's unalleged dust.

"Got a Kleenex?" I set the flamingo on the counter. He ducked down to look under the counter and that is when I grabbed the bird and took the stairs three at a time, having a little difficulty with the switch back. I hit the street. I crossed it. I headed for the beach, high-stepping it. I looked over my shoulder and damned if mutton-chops wasn't after me. What's more, the man could run. So many people in Marin County are marathoners and, except for thin, you can't tell by looking at them. Distance runners don't look like athletes. AIDS sufferers are thin, too, and so are anorexics and dopers. I'd have made him for a doper. This would be the second flamingo-owning marathoner I'd stolen from. Was there a connection? I, too, come to think of it, was a flamingo-owning marathoner, although ex in my case. That made three of us. I didn't know about Marie. She was thin all right, but fashionably so. French women don't race. The man had fooled me because I'd never once seen a mutton-chop-wearing runner. Didn't the stupidly-placed beard hair slow him down? It would me. But, no. He was right behind me.

Who was minding the store?

I ran through the town basketball court, the kiddy playground, past the Parkside burger stand, and tore through the picnic park to the beach, pouring it on, as we runners like to say. My knee was giving out on me. Both my body and I had forgotten that I couldn't run anymore, but at least the memory lapse had got us to the crowded beach. A howible pain shot through me as if someone took the kneecap and turned it like a doorknob. I was running in heavy sand now, to make matters not only worse, but totally impossible.

I sat down, really fell down, from the pain, scooped off my hat and glasses, buried them in the sand with the flamingo, wriggled out of my shirt, and lay down on top of this heap, face up, one hand over my eyes.

Through my fingers I saw Jack run by, stop, then look around. He was standing rather nearby. Wasn't he worried at all about leaving the shop untended, all his battered, broken, chipped, and filthy treasures lying there for the picking, jeopardizing them all for one lousy flamingo?

Maybe the bird was full of cocaine — or of diamonds, like the Maltese Falcon. Yes! This was the Maltese Flamingo sought by a cunning gang of international thieves and murderers. My life could be in danger. I wished it were.

After a while, Jack slumped off. I unburied the stuff, wrapped the flamingo in the shirt, resumed my glasses and cap, then went to join Joy and Nanny, having to limp over fifteen men, all of whom were playing with Joy to impress Nanny, who was reading Nietzsche. I never saw so many sand castles.

It wasn't until I was alone back at Jamie's house that I appreciated how ugly the bird was. Its wings were raised up for take off, or landing, or mating display, but it looked wholly unnatural and un-birdlike as if he were going to check for underarm odor. The wings were too straight and too black. The beak was too black, too, no yellow on it as there should be. And the pink color was actually fuchsia while the grass color was a ghastly turquoisey green, not looking like grass that would grow in volcanic mud or anywhere. It was produced by the same people who made the sugar and creamer, Sarsaparilla Deco Design, (made in Sri Lanka), the date, 1983, on the bottom as if to proclaim they were not trying to fake a fifties Art Deco original. It was tacky, tawdry, flamboyant, flashy, and garish.

The whole time I was running from Muttonchops, I forgot Jamie was dead.

VIII

FREE FLAMINGO

The five other partners bought George's shares. They were talking further expansion. I thought we'd expanded as far as possible. Anymore and we'd burst. Also, if we took the juice to the Midwest and east coast, how fresh was the juice going to be once it got there? How fresh was it now? To me, juice is fresh when you have just squeezed it and poured it into a glass, but who am I? Just the founder. The partners tell me that the man with vision, me, isn't necessarily the man that makes a company successful.

The company had gone ecoli conscious and although we thought that because of the high acidity content, ecoli wasn't a bacteria that could get into fruit, it could. All it had to do was fall from the tree into some animal poop. So we were being super safe. At the Vallejo plant there was an outside inspection and wash station, then the fruit got sorted and washed again. All our workers wore hair-covers, masks over their mouths, and rubber gloves.

Then, for super-safety, the juice got flash pasteurized, heated up and chilled down. Some argument here, on my part, about what that did to the freshness and nutrition, but who am I to be listened to? Just the founder. Then we had ongoing lab testing with our fruit safety experts. All this upped the overhead out of sight. The company was in debt.

So they wanted to go public, something I'd always been against, not wanting to be responsible for the public's money. Also, to me, going public was venturing into dangerous territory, the terrain of the hostile takeover. I'd already experienced two hostile takeovers – of my son and of my wife's womb.

If we were to go public, George would have done well to wait to sell his stocks until then and get double his millions but he was in a hurry. Part of the rush to go public no doubt was the other partners being anxious to recoup their outlay to George. There was to be a vote on it in a month.

Two weeks had passed since the Stinson Beach theft of Ugly and I'd run out of available flamingoes. I'd exhausted the local supply and was now taking entire days cruising antique stores and second hand stores of other towns. I'd even gone so far as to inquire of the shop-owners about flamingoes, drawing attention to myself thereby. Not a good idea. That's how I got stuck with the free flamingo and flamingo thieves don't accept flamingoes as gifts – that's one of the rules.

It was in a charming antique store in San Anselmo, a few towns north of Sausalito.

"Let me know if you are interested in anything," said a smiling, rosy-faced, young woman at the counter, the kind of woman I wanted for Zeus Juice ads instead of the hollow-eyed, attenuated models they chose whom they expected to appear healthy simply by standing them next to a bicycle.

This woman had blond, curly hair, sparkling eyes, and white teeth. She was probably our ad man's idea of fifty pounds overweight but she looked great to me.

"I was looking for flamingoes."

"China?"

"Well, yes, I guess, but any flamingo will do."

"I have a wooden flamingo."

"You do?" I didn't know if I was interested or not. I supposed I could be. Still, wood? It didn't seem right. What would the others in the *mat* say to this wooden sub species?

53

"It's been hanging around my van ever since I took it from my brother who didn't want it in his garden anymore. The legs broke off. Well, I'll take anything no matter how useless or broken. I can't help myself. That's why I started this store, so I could try to unload my stuff, give myself room to walk around my house. There are rooms I haven't been in for years for lack of a pathway. My garage? Don't ask — full to the rafters! As for my van, all the seats are covered with items, which will soon encroach onto the driver's seat. Then I'll just have to store the van and buy another. You'd be doing me a favor to take the flamingo."

I was listening with half an ear, wondering how to break into her van. Would I need a crowbar? Would I have to follow her home first and wait until darkness fell? This presented a real challenge. Things were looking up. The old heart was beating like a tom-tom.

"You can have it for free if you want it."

"No, no, I couldn't possibly," I said, experiencing genuine alarm.

"Believe me. I'm embarrassed to tell you how long it has been in my van and I'll never sell it in the store because I'll never fix the legs."

How could I explain that I only stole flamingoes and that she was wrecking everything by trying to give it to me? The more I protested, the more she thought I was just being nice.

"Hold on, I'll go and get it right now."

She told a woman who was busy with a feather duster to watch the store and also to watch me so I wouldn't go away. Then she trotted out the back door.

"Ordinarily Betsy would never give something away," the woman confided in me, looking troubled at Betsy's odd behavior. Despite her clutch of feathers, she was an unfortunate frog-like person, with bulging eyes and a receding chin.

"Ordinarily I never accept gifts," I confided back.

"Is that so?" She looked at me, torn between being impressed and puzzled. She ventured some information about herself. "I collect National Geographic magazines ..."

"Isn't that a hazard? I've heard of houses collapsing under their weight."

"I have a concrete bunker," she said, and I looked at her keenly to see if she was putting me on. "Anyhow, there was a June 1953 issue, I think it was, containing an article about flamingoes, you could have."

"No, thank you." I drew the line at flamingo ephemera. Also, was I to believe she had every issue's contents memorized?

She told me in detail about the article and it was, well, fascinating. I learned that the flamingo flies with its neck stretched out, unlike the heron and egret, whose neck, I'd noticed from the houseboat, is coiled when aloft. Flamingo chicks have straight beaks when born and are gray in color. Flamingoes honk when alarmed and the alarm cry was: huh huh huh. "And," she continued, "they are the only ones in the animal kingdom who do sieve eating."

"What about whales?" I asked, rather unkindly.

Like all information repeaters, she was thrown by a question that might require her to stop and think. Her head bobbled back and forth (head flagging?), but she recovered smartly and said, "They are the only bird or mammal that eat with their heads upside down in the water." She had me there. I was no match for froggy.

"Tell me, do you remember everything from every magazine in your collection or are you just interested in birds?"

"I remember everything I read," she said apologetically. "I can't help myself."

Everyone in this store couldn't help herself, including me.

The cute owner returned with a wooden flamingo two feet long. It had those teddy bear eyes where the pupil rolls around behind clear plastic. It was two dimensional, curvily carved out of a one-inch thick board. The legs were indeed broken off so we were just talking body, neck, and head. It was dirty and could have used more dirt to suppress its blaring pinkness. Twenty-four inches of pink is a lot and paint is different than glaze. I began to understand Stella's feeling about the color.

"This is really nice of you," I said when she forced it into my arms. "But, would you mind carrying it to my car for me. I'm embarrassed to be seen walking down the street with it." Especially in my red, flamingo-stealing shirt. Talk about clashing colors!

Both women laughed delightedly, thinking that I was joking then returned to busying themselves about the shop.

"I'm serious," I said. I was holding the flamingo down by my side, by the beak, in the most unobtrusive way I could.

"Well, this is good news, then," she said. "Now I know that you're not the flamingo thief."

"What? Who?"

"It happened over at Jack's shop in Stinson beach, Jack's Alleged Antiques, a couple of weeks ago. Jack, there, said some guy stole a flamingo, ran out of the shop, ran through the town, through all the parks, along the beach, all the while sort of holding this pink flamingo aloft like the Olympic flame."

I didn't in the least hold it aloft. Total nonsense. Muttonchops spreading stories. Trying to make me look like a fool just because I'd out-puppied him.

"You would have been too embarrassed to do that, right? Also, a real flamingo collector wouldn't want this broken, old, wooden thing."

"Were you testing me?" I asked, looking and sounding offended, since I was actually feeling offended, even hurt. I had thought she was being nice. I had thought she liked me, maybe was fantastically attracted to me.

"Well, I guess it was sort of a test," she admitted unremorsefully.

"I told you Betsy never gave stuff away," said Miss Memory from across the shop, relieved that her boss's uncharacteristic behavior was due to it being a nasty test.

Betsy smiled. "Come on, then, I'll carry it for you."

It turned out to be a lot more embarrassing, walking down the street with this chubby, rosy, woman conspicuously carrying the flamingo in her arms like a nursing baby than if I'd done my unobtrusive beak hold.

"What a beautiful car," she exclaimed as I hastily put the bird in the trunk.

"Would you like to go out with me some time?" I asked

"Are you married?"

"Yes."

"Good. I am, too. It's better if I see someone also married because they understand the difficulties. When shall we get together?"

"Now?"

"You just want to fuck me, right?"

"Yes." I tried not to look shocked at her forthrightness, the word fuck coming from someone so rosy. Also trying not to look shocked at my prompt assent.

"Well, there's nowhere to go. There's no room in your car. Or mine. Or in my house."

I was relieved to have gotten off this merry-go-round I'd launched myself on. Now I could gracefully say, too bad, goodbye, but instead my mouth asked, "Is your husband in your house?"

"No, he had to move. There wasn't room for him in the house because of my insane collecting, or in my bed because I got fat. We could have got a king-size bed, but ..." She shrugged.

"If you can fit your body in your bed and I'm on top of you, then it seems like I would fit, too." I looked around to see who was doing this talking, making these incredible proposals.

"Good point," she said amiably. "I like a man who's not easily daunted. Let's go and try."

Her house was large and as crowded as she'd promised. We threaded our way through to her bedroom. There was a path from the door to her bed but only half of the bed was usable because of a rampart of teddy bears on the other half. The lovemaking wasn't spectacular. I'd never been with a fat woman, or with any woman besides Stella in twenty years, and I was overcome by all the flesh, by not feeling any bones. I couldn't seem to find my way around. It was as if I were inside her trying to find my way out instead of the other way around. I could see why people referred to such episodes as adventures because it wasn't like sex so much as it was like traveling and getting lost. Also, it was a tight fit, us on the bed I mean, not me in her. That was actually a bit of a loose fit, but although I was a man who didn't daunt, my dick did daunt, and wasn't as puffed as it could be. It was the first time I'd worn a condom for one thing. After the pre-liminaries, she got on top of me for the big event and it was awesome how she loomed over me, and how her body rippled and swayed. She had an orgasm, making the flamingo alarm call, "Huh huh huh," which urged me on to my own orgasm.

I felt cheered. Even more so when she retrieved and opened a bottle of cold Muscatel, which we took out into her back yard to a pretty garden uncluttered by anything but nature and two chairs. Normally not a sweet wine drinker, this one hit the spot.

"Let's not tell each other our stories," she said.

"Good idea."

"I can see you are carrying some sadness."

"Right."

"It's funny you drive that car and at the same time wear those ripped pants."

Obviously she didn't want to tell her story, but was dying to hear mine, I thought, but then she reassured me, "You are a puzzle, but one I don't want to solve."

"I appreciate that. You have been so generous, Betsy – the flamingo, you, this delectable wine. I wish I could help you in some way about your overcrowded situation. It seems like we do things to make ourselves feel better, but at some point, it starts to invade our lives in such a way as to make us feel worse."

"So far, I'm still feeling better." She smiled.

"Even with your husband forced out?"

"Yes, it's a pleasure to visit him at his spacious, Zen-like house."

Maybe it was not unlike my situation at home. I think Stella enjoyed my calm, clean bedroom as long as she could go back to her stormy one when she wanted. Betsy wasn't stormy. She just had too many things. But they were neat, clean, organized.

I lifted my face to the sun, sipped the wine. Betsy seemed to be thinking about her mate. She said, "See, Tim, if he had tried to change me, the marriage would have gone to hell. Or if he had wanted to change me and made himself miserable by hoping I'd change. Oops, I'm telling my story. Anyhow, we all have to love each other for who we truly are, not for what we wish the other would be."

I needed to hear that because I was so heartbroken at the person Stella was now. After the night she had promised to speak more of Jamie, she still hadn't made one peep, even when I tried to draw it out of her. The fact was, we didn't talk about anything because she was rarely home. Or I was rarely home. When she was home with me, she was mad at me, or reading a book, or both. She was best when we were at parties, being affectionate to me in front of other people, which made me wonder if other seemingly happy couples in public deplored each other at home.

When Betsy and I said our farewells, she asked, "Why did you want a flamingo? You just don't seem the type."

"It was for my niece. Birthday coming up."

She laughed. "See, there is always a simple answer for everything. Jack and I and the other dealers have been baffled about that flamingo thief, why he'd go for that particular chintzy item, but maybe he, too, had a little girl to give it to. Still, why steal it? Why hold it aloft? Was he proud of what he had done?"

Damn Jack with his "aloft" lie.

"I'm going to make legs out of thin dowel rods, paint them yellow, and my niece can stick your flamingo in the garden outside her window. Goodbye, Betsy."

"Goodbye, Tim."

In Mill Valley, I got the materials at the hardware store, fixed and painted the bird's legs. I softened the pink blare and also detailed in some feathers, copying others in the *mat*, adding a little black here, a little yellow there, cream color, too. I was so proud of my flamingo retrofit, I stuck it on the front lawn of Jamie's house for the world to see. Why not? I hadn't stolen it. It was a gift. Then I went inside, changed my clothes, and had a cup of coffee in the flamingo cup I stole from my employee.

Later, walking up the dock, past all the wildly blooming pots of flowers the house-boaters had put by their gangplanks, I saw Stella walking ahead of me and hailed her. She asked me where I had been, which was an unusual question for her. We did not keep track of each other's whereabouts although we were generous in recounting our activities. Because we were college sweethearts, and knew each other inside and out, or used to, we trusted each other, no question, although now there should be a question, which maybe was why she was asking one.

"At work." I answered.

"This friend of mine had a bizarre sighting of someone she was sure was you, in San Anselmo, walking down the street with a chubby woman who was carrying a flamingo."

I unlocked the door and we walked in together, greeted by our great view, the descending sun coloring the sky, brightening the room. We had passed the vernal equinox and the sunset was inching away from the mountain. I slid open the deck door for the fresh breeze which was stirring up the lagoon as if it were a serious body of water.

"A real flamingo?" I asked.

Stella looked perplexed. "I'm having déjà vu, as if we'd had this conversation before. Yes, we did! About Arnold's stolen flamingo. How strange. There seems to be a flamingo theme in our life right now. And," she paused, assuming a thinking position, a la Rodin's *Le Penseur*, maybe because she had initiated French words into our conversation, "wasn't there another flamingo?"

She could not possibly know about any of the other myriad flamingoes in the new theme park of our life.

"Yes!" she clapped her hands. "Joy and her dead flamingo."

"But, Stella, that was a private conversation I had with Joy on the telephone," I exclaimed, wounded.

She threw herself down full length on the couch. "I listened in. Not purposely. The phone rang, I picked it up, and you had already answered. It was such a dear conversation that I kept listening. I'm sorry if it was wrong of me, but surely you and Joy don't have secrets from me. Bring me a glass of wine, will you?"

I did as she asked, pouring an ice water for myself.

"So, back to San Anselmo. I knew it wasn't you because when I asked what you were wearing, my friend said cargo pants and a red tee shirt." Stella laughed. "Impossible. Wrong man."

I smiled.

"But isn't it funny about all the flamingoes?"

"Very funny."

After dinner, leftovers and rice, Stella returned to her studio, which was a good thing because I had to go back to Mill Valley and remove the free flamingo from the lawn.

Stella wasn't home when I returned so I got ready for bed. I was thinking about Betsy, my first infidelity, so I wasn't paying attention to what I was doing. I took off my jeans and boxers, put them in the washing machine. I put the shirt in the laundry bag. Too bad I couldn't wash the cargo pants and red tee shirt, but I could at Jamie's house. I laid out my clothes for tomorrow, the usual blue jeans with white shirt, and I selected a belt and shoes, topsiders. Then I realized I'd done it in the wrong order. I always laid out my clothes for the next day first. Only afterward did I take off my present-day clothes.

I stood stock still, not knowing how to proceed. Should I get dressed again and do it right? I knew how stupid it was, but I also knew that I had to if I was going to be able to sleep. I resisted, but in the end, put tomorrow's clothes back in the closet, retrieved today's clothes from the laundry, re-dressed, laid out tomorrow's clothes then re-undressed. In this way my mind believed I was averting disaster.

"Well, James, things aren't looking too good. I'm losing it. And I don't seem to care. My behavior is, in a word, execrable. I hardly ever go to work. I sleep with strangers. I continue to steal flamingoes although I was thwarted today. Where will it end? In the grave, I guess, where everything ends, and nobody cares. The bad thing, though, is that the flamingo supply has dried up. I only have eight. I think I won't be happy until I have ten. Goodnight, James. I love you."

VIII

FLAMINGO NUMBER NINE

Zeus rhymed with juice. Otherwise he had nothing to do with squeezed fruit. In Ancient Greece, he was the supreme ruler, Lord of heaven and earth, Lord of the sky, rain-god and cloud-gatherer, flinging his thunderbolt to pierce open the sky. The early Zeus Juice ads, my ads, proclaimed that Zeus ruled! The supreme juice! Zeus lords it over all other juices!

Stella created a fantastic picture of Zeus throwing his thunderbolt and cracking open oranges and grapefruits so that they burst all over the sky, raining juice. This picture was on the trucks and labels and still is.

Back then we were living in a little house on the coast south of here, its rooms given over to crates of fruit and multitudes of juicers, the three of us sleeping in one room, the garage full of dishwashers thrumming away, cleaning glass bottles. I sold and delivered locally. Those were happy days. Well, all our days were happy days. It was exciting when Stella created the picture and we began to run ads and then got our first warehouse. We used to drive to the orchards to negotiate for the fruit ourselves, no middlemen. Eventually we got investors, first George then the others. And we grew and grew.

Stella never did another picture with those fabulous, bright colors, much as I urged her to. She said it was commercial, which of course it was, but it was so pretty!

Now her first show was coming up after working hard as an artist for twenty years, starting seriously at eighteen. I hoped with all my heart it would be a success, no one deserved it more, but, damn, she painted such gloomy subjects. Who would want them in their home?

It occurred to me to seed buyers at the show, backing them with my money, but it would kill Stella if she found out, and kill our marriage. She would never forgive me. It would be disrespectful of everything she stood for. However, I was afraid she might suffer such a huge disappointment that Jamie's death, which it seemed she'd managed to deal with through working hard at her art, would come crashing down on her again.

When the show was hung, she asked me to come over and see the paintings, just the two of us. The opening reception was the next night. She seemed extremely nervous. "You know it doesn't matter what I think," I said to her on the way to the Mill Valley gallery.

"It does to me."

When I got to the gallery, I saw why. The show was all about Jamie. It was her same theme of rooms, done in dark or muted colors, but there was light. Her light was so fine, it made up for the lack of color. From the room's windows, you could see a little boy running over a hill, bicycling down the drive, skateboarding on the sidewalk, always a small boy in the distance, and always going away from the house. Then there were pictures with no little boy, but something of his things in the room, not in the natural way that a boy would leave it, but in the way of a shrine with a flower, a candle, even a cross, along with the little boy object, some of which I recognized as things of Jamie's even though we didn't have them any more.

Stella held my hand as we went from picture to picture and the tears began to stream down my face. "The paintings are beautiful," I kept saying, "just beautiful. I am so proud of you."

Stella was crying now, too. We hugged each other hard. "Thank you, Tim. I'm so grateful. I was half-afraid you would be angry, that you'd feel I'd used Jamie, used his death."

"Not at all. You've incorporated it into your work in an inspiring way. And it has helped you. I can see that it has helped you to recover."

"It has. Tim, I felt in such constant touch with Jamie while I worked, almost as if he were guiding my brush. Like you must feel when you talk with him before sleep."

But I didn't feel that way. I talked to him out of my own need but he wasn't there. He wasn't in the room or in me. He never answered. He was gone. Totally, irrevocably gone.

Stella had taken our child's death and out of her terrible loss, created art, possibly great art. I was deeply moved and I was glad for her – for the process that gave her Jamie back, and for the creations that evolved. This was an intimate, important, healing moment for us.

But it all turned around for me the next night at the reception. Stella looked beautiful in a simple white dress and red silk shawl with fringes. Her skin was tanned even browner and her hair was so bright it practically cast reflections. There was a banner raised which read Stella Ramirez, her maiden name.

Red dots were going up beside the pictures, the subtle proclamation of a sale, and there was a huge crowd. Critics were there from the *San Francisco Chronicle* as well as local papers.

I drifted around to listen to the talk and it was all about the content, about "the artist's death in the family ..."

"... her little boy, Jamie."

"... so young ..."

"... such a tragedy ..."

And I began to get angry at the paintings for putting my lost son's name in the viewers' uncaring mouths, and angry with Stella, too. First of all, Jamie had not been little when he died. He had been a strapping thirteen-year-old. Why had she portrayed him as a small boy? Was it to milk more sympathy? It began to seem to me that she, who had deplored commercial art, was in fact commercializing his death in a horrid way, sentimentalizing it. Our devastating loss had become a comic strip, which people were avidly enjoying and cheerfully discussing between sips of wine and bites of cheese, while Stella, looking like a gypsy dancer, was the center of attention, the belle of the ball, the star, luxuriating in her success, surrounded by admirers.

All that I had hoped for her show had come to pass and here I was being a sorehead, a sorehead afraid of what he might do, how he might act out and ruin it all for her. George was in a circle of people, and I pulled him away. "Tell Stella I got sick and had to go, that I can't make it to the dinner after. Tell her I'm sorry. Stomach flu."

"But are you okay, Ears? Do you want me to come away with you, drive you home?"

"No. She should have family with her. I really do feel sick." I did. When I stepped outside, I vomited on the sidewalk.

I went across the street to the Book Depot and got a cup of tea. My stomach settled. I didn't want to go home and I certainly didn't want to go back to the show. What I wanted to do was go to the orgy house and try again to lose myself in sensation. I'd considered this on and off for the last couple of weeks, but I wasn't sure I remembered where it was. I didn't know if the orgy happened every night or only on certain nights. Possibly it became the flogging club on alternate nights and I didn't want to blunder into that without a Viking helmet.

Also, if I found the correct place on the correct night, I didn't know what the password was, or how much money to pay. I could have asked

George for all this information, but I didn't want him feeling he'd sent me on the path to degradation. He had only been trying to cheer me up that one night.

I got in the Boxster and drove down the canyon. I knew it was on the right side, and I knew it was set back from the road, up a driveway. There were only a few possibilities. I narrowed it down to one house, which was the only one that looked familiar. I parked, walked up the driveway, then up a flagstone path to the front door. Had there been a flagstone path? Were there hydrangeas? My memory was hazy. I had been halfway drunk from the beer drinking that night.

I rang the doorbell. A handsome young boy answered. He was friendly. "Hi, come on in," he said, as if expecting me, as if I didn't need a password. I followed him in. This was not the house. No music, no dim lights, no other people nude or dressed, except for a younger boy who was sitting in the kitchen, the room to which I was led.

I don't know why I kept following, kept penetrating the house which was not the right house. I should have told him at the door that I had made a mistake. But he was so friendly and I needed a friend.

"You're here for Mom, right?" he inquired over his shoulder.

I still didn't speak. It was as if I were in a dream. I looked at the two boys, one fourteen years old, one about sixteen or seventeen. They were dark and slight, part Asian. The younger boy wore glasses and had some curl to his hair. I knew him. He was Paul Barnes.

He said unhappily, "Hi, Mr. Forester."

I sat down at the kitchen table, feeling dizzy, hoping I wasn't going to vomit again. I put my head between my knees.

"Are you okay?" Paul's brother brought me a glass of water.

"It is Jamie Forester's Dad," Paul told his brother in a ghastly voice.

"Oh, no!" His brother groaned. He sat down and drank my water.

A woman entered the kitchen, dressed for the evening, but looking a little frazzled. Lisa Barnes. She was Japanese, short, maybe less than five feet. She had a boyish haircut and a sweet face. "Aren't you early?" she said as she entered. "Or am I late?" I raised my head from my knees. She looked at me and turned pale. "Oh!"

"It's Mr. Forester," the boys said in unison, looking horrified. "Jamie's dad."

"Oh, dear." She sat down. Now we were all looking sick.

"We were expecting you or your lawyer that first month," she said, "and the second month. But you never came. And then we hoped ... Oh, Mr. Forester, we were wrong not to come to you. But Jimmy, our James, felt so bad, so guilty, so scared ..."

"I'm sorry, Sir," said their James.

"I wanted him to tell you how sorry he was, how sorry we all were," his mother said, "but I thought to apologize might be to admit blame and so I wanted to protect Jimmy, keep him hidden and out of your mind. We were so afraid you might sue us for all we had. Or even that Jimmy might be prosecuted."

I started to cry.

"Oh, my god," she said. She got me a glass of water and put it beside the water glass Jimmy had given me drunk from himself. Then she went to the fridge and got a bottle of wine and poured us both a glass of that. I got a handkerchief from my pocket. It smelled of vomit from wiping my mouth with it earlier. I blew my nose and dabbed my eyes. I drank some water and then some wine. "I'm sorry," I said.

This was definitely not the orgy house.

"No, no, it's all right, it's okay," they all said.

"I'm glad you came," Jimmy said. "It's been the most horrible year waiting. Now you are here."

I felt like he was putting his wrists out to be handcuffed, or laying his head on the block.

"Please don't be worried," I assured all stricken three of them. I only came by because … because I wanted to see a friend of Jamie's. I wanted to see Paul. It's not about the accident. I never blamed you. Never."

I remembered the house now, the driveway where it happened. That's why the house had seemed familiar. How strange that I had ended up here. What a good thing it was that I did.

"My wife is an artist. She had an opening of a show downtown tonight and the paintings were all about Jamie. They were about her feelings. Well, it upset me. I left the gallery, and then I came here, not really knowing where I was going." (Man, that was the truth.) I smiled. "I'm glad I ended up here with you all, glad that I found you."

They smiled with me. Jimmy laughed aloud with relief. "Please stay for supper with us." The doorbell rang. "There's my date. I'll get rid of him."

We had spaghetti al pesto with salad. Lisa was a vegetarian and the boys complied, she said, every other night. Paul, after some encouragement, reminisced about Jamie and I felt happy hearing the stories, discovering little adventures in Jamie's life I hadn't known about. It was a wonderful evening. Lisa's husband had divorced her and I could not imagine how her husband had given them all up. Where was he? What could he have elsewhere that could be any better than this? I wanted to beg them to take care of each other, protect each other from harm. Except that you can't. You can't always be with them when danger comes. And even if you are, a boy can die while you sleep.

On the table, next to the salt and pepper, jam jar, and vase of daisies, was a flamingo toothpick-holder, only a little bigger than Uno. Without stealth of any sort, I put it in my pocket before I left. It was quite possible that one or all of them saw me do it, but no one said anything. For a year they had feared I was going to take them for everything they had so what did a toothpick-holder matter?

IX

FLINTSTONE

The critical response to Stella's show was good. They praised her light. One compared her to a Dutch master. She had sold five out of the twelve paintings and the show would be hanging for another month. The gallery owner said she would sell them all. A San Francisco gallery had offered her a show in eight months. She'd hit big time and was flying high.

I did not tell her about my revulsion of feeling regarding her work. Let her be happy. I didn't tell her anything about my life these days, about who I saw, what I did. She knew nothing and didn't seem to care.

I did not tell her that I had been asked to resign as CEO of Zeus and that if I didn't resign I'd be fired. Except for my "Story" benefit, how I'd started the company from nothing, I was a negative influence, in the way, of no use. I didn't care. I hated everything about Zeus Juice now.

I would still be on the board of directors because of my large stock holdings, but I would not be calling any of the shots. I'd lost my company. When it went public, I could hostilely take it back, but I didn't want it anymore. I didn't care. I'd rather sell apples from a truck. Or blimeys.

There was a guy on the dock, a Brit, who used to captain an inter-island cargo boat in the Caribbean. Captain Rick had crossed a lime with a honeydew melon, a nearly impossible feat, as one was a citrus fruit from a tropical tree, the other a vine-growing cucurbitaceous fruit. He started them in a makeshift greenhouse, then grew them on his deck in pots. They grew like limes do in ongoing cycles whereby flowering, fruiting, and ripening were all going on at the same time in all stages rather than, like melons, having just one harvesting period. They were softball size, green, smooth-skinned, flavorful, with high tang effect, overflowing with juice.

The flower itself was gorgeous to behold, yellow as a melon flower, perfumed as a lime blossom. The man was a genius.

I had told Rick that I would like to take them to market, that I'd buy some acreage in the Sonoma Valley and we could grow them in bulk. He maintained they could only be grown on the floating houseboats, in pots, caressed by Sausalito sun, wind, and fog, organically, with love.

There was no Sausalito water acreage available for sale. "Okay, then," I told him. "We'll both grow them on our decks and sell them for a thousand dollars apiece to the Japanese. Maybe as a further inducement, we can say that every fiftieth blimey could kill them, like the blowfish they love to eat that is incomparably delicious, but if ill prepared, poisons one to death, a fatality they're willing to risk, adding zest to the dining experience. They would never know which one is the fiftieth blimey. Sort of like the ninth wave, the one that engulfs you while you are standing on the beach watching the sunset while the other waves had just lapped at your toes."

But Captain Rick, who lived on a modest tugboat, wasn't interested in gain. He must have had a missing gene. So we simply ate them as fast as we grew them, sharing them with other docksters. Like pears, they had window of perfect ripeness that was about half an hour.

Every morning I watered my blimeys. I was going to put in a drip watering system but the Blimey Master nixed that idea, maintaining they had to be hand watered because it was while watering you got in touch with them, scrutinized them for bugs, ill health, mild depression. It was then you admired them (they loved praise) and also judged how much water they needed according to the current weather. The Captain also ordered that every week or ten days we had to read them Kipling, and to drink rum while we did it. George was always invited to Blimey Night. He was the best reader.

"Are you coming to Blimey Night," I asked him on the phone, "Or is this your Transsexual Club Night?"

"We like to call it the Transgender Club."

"Of course."

"But I'm giving all that up. As the Buddha says, *Desires are insatiable. I vow to end them.* I thought that if I went to the limit with sex, I'd put an end to being driven by my desires, but I only whetted them. I only became a pervert. Also, satisfaction, such as it is, lasts no more than forty seconds and I hate myself afterward."

George sounded serious, but I kept up our usual playful tone. "It struck me you were having fun."

"Well, that, too."

"So now you are going Buddhist."

"Yes, a monk. But I have a lot to learn first. I have to make a lot of changes."

"I'll bet." Was he serious? I didn't know. He probably didn't know either. "Where are you calling from, home, hospital, or hermitage? Is Laurie listening?"

"I'm home."

"Can Joy play?"

"Don't you work anymore?"

I told him what had happened at Zeus. He blamed himself. I soothed him. I told him about my disenchantment with the company, with the new regime. I would have liked to tell him I was happy enough growing blimeys and stealing flamingoes. It struck me that blimey was sort of flamingo spelled backward, or at least a distant relative. Mark Twain once said, not exactly on point, that, *"Cauliflower is nothing more than cabbage with a college education."*

George said Joy could play so I picked her up in the Boxster and drove to the Steins to play with Flintstone, the bulldog puppy. Marie had said there would be someone to let us in. I believe she could have added, 'so you don't have to break in this time,' because Marie seemed all-seeing, all-knowing — especially about me, not just because she pumped George, which I knew she did (and he was eminently pumpable), but because she was intuitive, something all psychiatrists should be, but so rarely were.

Flintstone was growing fast, but mostly sideways. Joy and I took him for a walk, or a prolonged pee. He must have peed fifty times. He put his mark on everything, every stone and leaf, every tree trunk, hydrant, and bush. This zigzag trudge was Joy's kind of walking. I controlled my impatience with both of them. I was a man who liked a destination whether I was biking, kayaking, or walking, and I liked to move fast and straight ahead. But what was the hurry after all? Where were we trying to get? Nowhere. We were playing. Still, I wished I were a smoker. Marijuana would be a sympathetic product for this zigzag trudge.

Then Joy decided we had to take Flintstone for a drive with the top down so we did. He was not a typical dog who loves to put his face in the wind. (Why do dogs do that?) Instead he cowered down on the floor by the passenger seat. Maybe you need a proper snout to face into the wind. Bulldog faces look like they've been formed in the wind at gale force and they probably feel that any more wind would rearrange their features beyond recall.

"I think we are making Flintstone miserable. Let's take him home."

"To the houseboat, Uncle Tim?"

"Back to the Steins."

Marie was just getting home. She made me a cup of coffee and I noticed she had not replaced her sugar and creamer. "How are you doing, Tim?"

Probably she had heard about my running from Stella's show to vomit on the sidewalk. Maybe she had seen me.

"Not very well, but I had fun just now with Flintstone and Joy. Thanks for letting us play."

"If you think of seeing a therapist, I could advise you. There are anti-depressants…" She let the word hang in the air like a kite I could reel in or let go.

"Stella takes them but I don't want to. I don't want to muffle my grief. It's not fair."

"Not fair to whom?"

I was quiet. I didn't know whom it wasn't fair to. I didn't know what I meant.

Marie had sparkling eyes, but they were different from Betsy's. Marie's was a smart sparkle, which should have turned into a glint, but didn't. Betsy's eyes said Oh boy! Stella's, non-sparkling, were deep pools, eyes to fall into, whence to happily drown.

"Are you glad Stella feels better?"

"Yes."

"She would like you to feel better, I'm sure. So would all your loved ones, including Jamie."

"I have moments."

"When?"

"When I do something exciting."

"Adrenaline is an anti-depressant."

"Really? I didn't know that. Then that's partly it."

"Do you feel bad after these exciting moments? Do you feel you've been unfair to Jamie?"

"No, because I feel the excitement is keeping me alive and I have to keep alive so as to keep grieving for him. So someone will."

Was that what the flamingo stealing was all about?

Not really, as George would say.

Marie thought about what I'd said, then smiled gently. "Good."

Despite her sparkling eyes, ready smile, sexy body, and fluffy hair, she was the most serious person I'd ever known.

As we said goodbye, and I tore Joy away from Flintstone, Marie said, "Think about fortitude."

Back at the houseboat, Joy asked if she could spend the night.

"Sure, honey. You can sleep in my room. I'll sleep with Stella. Or you can sleep with Stella and me. Also, your dad is coming for Blimey Night. Maybe he'll stay over, too."

"Where did Jamie sleep?"

"We didn't have this boat when Jamie was alive. We lived in Mill Valley near you. Remember the yellow house?"

"Sort of."

She didn't. It killed me that she didn't remember.

We were downstairs looking at my room. Catty-corner to it was a half room that served as a home office for me. "This can be my room," said Joy, stepping into it, claiming it. "Let's fix it up."

The next hour we spent inventing a little girl's bedroom. I shoved my desk into the corner and put my filing cabinet under it. Since Stella was a pillow maniac, we could take from her surplus to fashion a small bed. From the linen closet, I got a flowered sheet and tacked it over the window for a curtain. Joy spotted an African violet plant in the kitchen and brought it down, the pot clattering against the saucer as she walked. From the bathroom, she took a hooked rug with a picture of a fish on it to put by her bed.

I plugged in a small lamp. She was all set. We took a nap together on the tiny, rumpled bed to get ready for Blimey Night.

Blimey Night began on our deck where we cooked hamburgers and vegiburgers on the grill, the sun making a simple sunset of it, coloring the water where ducks, coots, and a lone Canadian goose paddled around the birds which never paddled, only bobbed, these being mostly the gulls.

For dessert, we went on to Captain Rick's tugboat. George, Joy, Rick and I, sat out on the slanting deck among the potted blimeys under the gentle stars. I was surprised he hadn't insisted I put my planters on a slant like his were, proclaiming that to be an essential position for growing and successful fruiting, along with fog, hand watering, pot planting, and Kipling reading.

Because Joy was with us, we read Kipling's, *How the Elephant Got His Trunk*. George was the reader. I let my mind wander. The blimeys paid attention, perked up their leaves.

I thought about fortitude and didn't come up with anything except that it began with F and had the same amount of syllables as Flamingo. So did Forester for that matter. Fortitude made me think of folks like Arctic explorers. What had it to do with me? Well, it was about bearing up, I guessed, in the face of hardship, of suffering. I did not look like a suffering person, sitting here, drinking rum with buddies, and they didn't look like sufferers either, but who knew what George suffered, or Rick, or even little Joy?

Maybe Marie was saying that fortitude to one degree or another was how everyone got through misfortune, through life itself, or just through each day, that it was there for us all to call upon, instead of Prozac or adrenalin, drugs or booze. Perhaps all those products allowed fortitude to rust, made it less bright and available. She was saying you don't have to be an Arctic explorer because fortitude is in everyone, part of the original package.

Joy fell asleep and, as George carried her down the dock, I told him that she had hoped to spend the night on the houseboat. He paused at my gangplank. "Not tonight. She might wake up and be frightened, not know where she is. Better not."

I wanted to tell him that we had made a special little room for her and that he could spend the night, too, but it would sound like begging. So I called up a scrap of fortitude and said, "Good night, then." Cheerfully. I kissed Joy's sublime little forehead. I kissed George, too.

"'Night, Ears."

Back in the boat, I looked sorrowfully at Joy's room. It had been such fun getting it all ready. But we'd just been playing. Stella called from her bedroom, "After your ritual, come sleep with me. See what it's like fucking a famous artist."

I did and it was nice.

X

FAULT

Stella went right off to her instant sleep while I stared at the ceiling and listened to the thrumming of the Toadfish.

Yes, it was nice having sex with Stella and I got George's forty seconds of satisfaction, but that is not what sex with my wife is about for me. It's about reconnecting, reuniting. Every time, for me, our sex together is saying, remember us? We're a pair. We belong together. We love each other until the end of time.

We hadn't had a lot of lovemaking this summer. My birthday night was the most memorable. Soon after that, Stella told me her grim news and I hadn't felt the same about her, didn't feel the same desire.

Tonight she seemed different, like a woman who maybe had experienced sex with someone else and had done special things he'd asked for and now, maybe not consciously, was seeing how I liked these same things.

So I stared at the ceiling and wondered if she had a lover. All those nights working late at the studio ...

Would I care? My stance with Stella was – anything that helped, anything to help her get through the grief, because I knew how bad it was, and how one grasped at straws. It was okay to do anything that could make her forget and be happy for a minute. So, if a lover could do that for her, hooray!

As long as she didn't leave me. She was all I had left. In her I had Jamie's entire history and most of my own history. The idea of my living with anyone who hadn't intimately known and loved our son was inconceivable. I had to be able to say, "Remember when Jamie...?"

But did I say that? When did I even see Stella to say that these days? When we saw each other, we said things like, "Did you remember to get the milk?" Or she talked about her art, endlessly, and I sat there not telling her about what was happening to me, that I'd lost my company, and now stole flamingoes for a living.

She was Jamie's mother. I loved her no matter what. She could have ten lovers.

What about Betsy? She was not a lover. She was a kindness. I had no intention of being with her again and it wasn't because of all the teddy bears and piles of furniture I feared might come toppling down on us if we shook the bed too hard, and it wasn't her unaccustomed fleshiness, which I'd found endearing and welcoming after the initial strangeness, it was that I didn't want a lover. I wanted Stella. Forever.

The next day was Saturday, and I was going to Petaluma, an hour north, to an Art Deco auction. One of the antique store people had told me there was a good chance to find a flamingo at that auction. I knew I should exercise first, bike or kayak, but I only wanted to get in the car and speed my way up 101 north. It would be nice of me to ask Stella if she wanted to bike or kayak, but I didn't want to ask her. If she asked me, I would say yes and go, but otherwise I'd hit the road, get lunch in Petaluma by the river, and fool around until auction time.

After a blueberry pancake breakfast, Stella said, "If you'll vacuum the upstairs, I'll vacuum the downstairs."

This was fair. Upstairs was more furniture to move, but downstairs was predominately her room, the messiest. In a burst of good feeling, I said, "I'll vacuum the whole boat." We could have a cleaning lady, but the boat was small, about 1200 square feet, and all our lives, we had wanted to do our own cleaning. It felt right.

"Okay, I'll wash the kitchen and bathroom floors." She put our breakfast dishes in the washer and went to work wiping the counters.

She was wearing white linen pants and a sky blue tee shirt. She never wore tee shirts with logos, but, unlike me, went for color. Her hair was pulled back in a ponytail, which didn't suit her. It made her face look too sharp. "What are you going to do about your office?" she asked.

When I looked blank, she said, "The art installation you and Joy made yesterday."

It griped me that she called Joy's room an art installation. "I'll just keep it like that for now," I said calmly, "for when she comes again."

"I don't think you should, Tim."

"Why not? Maybe I'll take out my desk and files and then it can be her room entirely."

"Tim, Joy is not your child. I really don't think it is good that you spend so much time with her. Now this."

Now what? What the hell was she talking about? My throat closed up. Here I had said (in my mind) that she could have ten lovers and she begrudged me playing with my niece. "Are you jealous of Joy?" I got out hoarsely.

She colored. "Of course I'm not. What an idea!"

I swallowed a few times and my voice began to take on volume and tone. "Maybe you wish I would spend more time with you, but you have been so busy getting ready for your show, working day and night, night after night." I looked to see if she would blush again, and she did. She was not an easy blusher because of her dark skin and tough nature.

She would not be diverted, however, and continued with the subject of Joy. "I don't think it is healthy. You are getting too hung up on Joy."

"Hung up? Listen to you. I love Joy, if that's being hung up."

"I just don't want you being hurt. What if George and Laurie moved away? What if Laurie left George and took Joy?"

Scared, my heart hammered. "Do you know something I don't?"

"No."

"Am I to spend the rest of my life not loving anyone for fear I will lose them?" She didn't answer, looked away. "Is that what you are going to do?"

"Probably."

"Are you going to stop loving me so that when I die, you won't care?"

"Maybe."

My heart melted. "Oh, Hon!" I took her in my arms. "You'll only make yourself sadder or, worse, unfeeling and mean. We have to have love in us. That's all there is, all that is important. No sense in living otherwise."

"There is art."

"Yes. But I think it is the feeling in your work that is making it so successful right now, don't you?"

She laughed. "You mean it's true, that old chestnut about artists should suffer?"

"Right. But I don't see why juice kings should. Where's the vacuum? I'm hot to clean."

I started in her room, which had achieved the proportions of outright squalor. How could anyone live like this? Dirty clothes were everywhere although the washing machine or laundry basket was only a step away. There were dirty plates and glasses, dead flowers in slimy vases. Art books, disrespected, were open, marked, torn, dirty. There was paper trash, the papers that accrue in one's daily life that the normal person disposes of by tossing or filing or attending to. She was almost like one of those people you see whose cars are full to the gunwales with clutter and you can only shake your head wonderingly. She must not see what is around her. But how can an artist not see? Maybe she was always looking into her mind. In her own person she was clean, neat, pretty as a picture. Her studio was well organized. Anyone meeting her would never believe her room looked like this.

I attacked it with zest. It was one of those cleaning projects where a massive difference could be made and was therefore satisfying. Stella did not feel guilty about my cleaning it because she knew that I, a clean freak, was glad to take on the Herculean task of cleaning the Augean stable. She felt she was doing me a favor.

She was long gone by the time I finished my job. I showered, got into summer clothes of khaki shorts, white tee shirt, a narrow, tooled, leather belt, sandals. It would be hot in Petaluma.

Before I hit the highway, I went to Mill Valley to see George. Stella had scared me. I had to know that everything was all right. With George behaving so erratically, it could easily not be.

Laurie came to the door. "Hi, Tim, come in. I suppose you've come to play, but Joy is out with George." Laurie was in the midst of watching a golf game. She always watched a little longingly, knowing she could be out there playing with the pros if she hadn't been a good girl and gone to law school. She put it on mute and turned to me. I sat down next to her on the couch.

"Laurie, I'm sorry if I'm meddling into personal matters, but Stella gave me a terrible scare this morning suggesting all might not be great with you and George."

She turned off the game. "Please repeat the conversation," she said. Lawyer.

I did as she asked.

Laurie shook her head. "That bitch."

"What!" I was shocked. "Wait a minute."

"Tim. Spare me. Don't defend her. Can't you see her for what she is? I know she's grieving. I know she's had a terrible time, blah, blah, etc., etc. But she was a bitch before Jamie died and she's ten times worse now. I probably don't know the half of it. George told me about her operation, and her not telling you first. Christ almighty!"

I kept saying, "Wait," but she vocalized over me.

"But this takes the cake. The one happiness in your life right now, the fun you have with Joy, she's trying to take away from you, or make you feel bad about. It's sick."

I stood up. I couldn't hear this. "Please ..."

"And you know what it is really all about, don't you? I promised George I'd never say this, but I'm going to. I have to. I'm sick of pretending. I'm sick of everyone thinking poor Stella. And now this disgusting art show of hers ..."

"What? No, don't tell me. I don't want to hear it." I headed for the door.

"Jamie's death," she called after me. "It was her fault."

I stopped in my tracks, turned. "You're crazy. How could the accident be Stella's fault?"

"We were all at the hospital. In emergency, remember?"

"Yes."

"And Jamie was fine. No concussion. Nothing broken."

"Yes?" I walked back across the room to where she sat. Her voice was softer now. I had to come closer.

"But the doctor said Jamie should spend the night at the hospital. For observation."

"I don't remember ..."

"George said so, too. And naturally you agreed. But Stella, in her typical bossy way, said no. He was better off at home. The hospital was only minutes away, she said. Jamie was better off with her, she said, with his mother. You fought about it. You tried to keep Jamie there. But she won. As usual. You've always done whatever Stella wants."

I sat down again. "Good God! I wonder if she remembers."

"Has she never mentioned it?"

"Never. But don't you see how, if she does remember, it makes it even worse for her, Laurie. She'd have that gigantic guilt on top of the grief."

"Except she's doing just fine, and you are not."

"Why are you saying all this? Do you think I should leave Stella?"

"I think it would be a great idea."

"It crossed my mind last night and I said to myself that I never could. She's all that I have. She's Jamie's mother."

"Don't say that. You have us. We are your family every bit as much as she is and we remember Jamie, too. Do you know that George has asked me in all seriousness if we could give you Joy?"

"Did you say yes?"

Laurie laughed and hugged me. "I came close."

Driving to Petaluma, top down, weather getting warmer mile by mile, I considered Laurie's words. She was always one to go overboard in her judgments, but suppose she was right about Stella? When a woman is your college sweetheart and you've loved her as long as I have Stella, you always see her and think of her as she was at first.

She could have been turning into a bitch without me noticing or with me always making allowances. It's true that I gave into her on a lot of things. It seemed the easier way and it was no problem, really. But to others she might seem like a tyrant. It made me want to rush to her studio and look at her with fresh eyes. But I knew I would simply see the Stella I had always loved and would always love, come what may.

As for the hospital scene, the shock of Jamie's death must have blanked it out of my mind and, mercifully, out of Stella's mind, too. At home, that night, one or the other of us had been sitting by Jamie all through the night while unbeknownst to us the blood clot was moving inexorably to his heart.

At dawn, the evil, life-taking darkness being wafted away by sunlight and birdsong, Jamie sleeping peacefully, we went to bed, slept deeply at last, awaking around ten to a dreadful stillness that made us tumble from the bed and race to Jamie's room where his body was already cold.

I stopped thinking as I arrived in Petaluma. I had lunch by the river and chatted with a cheerful old couple. They had come from San Francisco by boat, tying up at the restaurant and planned to mosey down the Delta for a week's vacation, docking at various harbors.

After coffee, I got back in the car and sought out the fairgrounds. It wasn't until I parked that I realized Laurie had not reassured me about her and George.

XI

FINAL FLAMINGO

I'd never been to an auction before. Stella was the purchaser of the family (if we can still be a family with only two of us) and she always bought new, even when we were starting out, completely broke, all our monies invested in the business. She didn't like to think of things having belonged to others before her. She'd rather do without.

Petaluma is the egg capital of the world, renowned also for its pretty Victorian houses and annual arm wrestling championship, or wrist wrestling as they call it, but I like arm. It turns out to have a lot of antique stores, too, and out of that evolved periodic auctions. The fairgrounds were gala with flags, booths, and tents. Under the biggest tent was the Art Deco auction. Of the lots to be sold: tables, chairs, and bureaus predominated, many made of a golden, birds-eye maple that was popular for the period, forties and fifties, but still looking modern even in the gateway of year 2K. Art Deco design ranged from lovely and amusing to absolutely ghastly, the lamps particularly.

I stood bemused before some home bars decked out in chrome and glass and curvy lines that were terrific, although nowadays you'd be embarrassed to have such a flamboyant drinking statement in your home. One simply brings a bottle down from the kitchen cupboard. Sets of martini shakers and glasses were big then, too, as well as round mirrors, gaudy pictures with mirrored frames, vases of bizarre shapes and colors. It all verged on bad taste, but ended by being joyful. There were some fantastic, little, variously-colored radios designed so sweetly and whimsically it broke your heart to think of the sterile, gray, obnoxiousness of today's high tech equipment.

There were two flamingoes, a matched set, and they were not pocket size, briefcase size, or even suitcase size. They were life size, five feet tall, made of plaster, but covered with what looked like many coats of paint and varnish so they had an alabaster smoothness and gleam. One stood with head curled up, the other with head curving down, Dagwood style. As with all of the flamingoes I'd seen, they stood in long grass (these ones being more like fronds) — the reason being that their long skinny legs would be too breakable were they not supported by the added thickness of pseudo grass, mud dwellers though they preferred to be. Too bad that no one ever fashioned a flamingo sitting on its volcanic mud nest, legs folded. I'd have liked one of those.

But these two statues captured my heart. They were beautiful, even had a certain nobility bordering on arrogance, more the eagle's affect than the silliness or flightiness one attaches to flamingoes (one being me). I looked carefully and there was nowhere a chip. The pink was particularly fine with a lavender sheen and the bits of black on the wing feathers were painted with a restrained hand. The beak and eyes were black, and so were the toenails.

I wondered how much they weighed. Was it permissible to ascertain the heft of items before the bidding? For a flamingo thief, price was no object, but weight was. Size was, too. Clearly I was not going to nab one of these big boys from the site. The theft would have to be from the buyer.

I wrapped my arms around one of the pair and lifted it slightly off the ground. It was probably about fifty pounds.

My heart pounded percussively as, over the back of the statue, I saw Muttonchops looking at me from about ten feet away. Did he recognize me? Too bad he happened to spy me with a flamingo in my arms. Was he thinking, Let's see you hold this one aloft, you son of a bitch?

I was wearing shorts. He knew my legs. His legs had chased them, stride for stride. Carefully I set the flamingo back down.

"I suppose if you buy it, I'll have to carry it to the car for you so you won't be embarrassed."

It was Betsy. Betsy, looking adorable in a sleeveless flowered dress, with a low V neck, attire Stella wouldn't be caught dead in, but which looked delightful on Betsy, here on the Petaluma fairgrounds.

Now my hammering heartbeat changed to a pleasurable, non-anxious excitement, a thump, thump, thump, as the memory of our lovemaking assailed me and, strangely, even though it hadn't occurred to me to meet with her again, she looked as desirable to me as she had at first meeting. My cock forgot all about the teddy bears and how appalled I was when threading my way through the serpentine maze of her dementedly over-crowded house.

Then Muttonchops fetched up beside us, telling Betsy, "This is the guy."

"What guy?" I asked him, challenging him on the spot, frowning at him for his impertinence, presuming to nail me in front of Betsy for the theft of his lowly, dust-covered statuette worth ten bucks max.

Betsy was flustered. "The flamingo guy?" she asked him. "No way. This is a friend of mine. Jack, this is Tim."

Momentarily, Jack looked uncertain, but then stoutly said, "He's the guy who stole my flamingo."

Since Betsy had told me about the theft of Jack's flamingo, I couldn't pretend ignorance, so I just said, "I'm not the guy." Frostily.

"Jack, I told you he's my friend, so lay off." I liked her for her loyalty, for her springing to my defense, no questions asked. Her outstandingly friendly face now looked positively pugnacious.

"How many six-foot-tall, blond guys are there who like flamingoes? With big ears," he added, unnecessarily I thought. He himself was about five eight with dark hair and, I have to say, quite nice ears.

"Flamingoes with big ears?" I asked, only to annoy.

Betsy laughed and Jack smiled a little.

"Tell me about these little radios." I walked away from the telltale flamingoes. "How much will they go for?"

"Forget it," Betsy said. "They cost between fifteen hundred and two thousand dollars each."

"That's nothing for him," Jack said, following us. "I recognize him now. He's not the flamingo thief, he's the Juice King. I saw his picture in the paper last week. Business page. That's probably why he looked familiar."

Was Jack capitulating? Why would he think a Juice King and a flamingo thief were mutually exclusive? "Ex-Juice King," I explained to him, although I supposed I should talk to him through Betsy as he was doing to me, as if I were no longer there. "That's why the picture was in the paper — to tell the world."

"Yeah, it's the shits. A guy builds up his own company and some assholes come along and take it away." He spoke like a man who had experienced the same thing, himself, time and time again, although as a profession he simply presided over the dirtiest junk shop in Northern California.

The auction commenced and we got our numbered paddles in return for our names, then we took our seats, Betsy and I together, Jack drifting away, thank God. As the auctioneer started to rap out his first description, I realized I was worried about Betsy adding to her already vast accumulation, and said as much.

"I'm just here to buy smalls," she said. "That's the term for little items, even though I don't go in for them much in my store. And Art Deco isn't my style. I'm a Country kind of gal. Still, auctions are fun. If you want me to bid for you, let me know. Sometimes a buyer likes to remain secret."

Betsy left before I did, having bought totally non-smalls in the form of a dressing table, stool to go with it, two lamps, three vases, four matching chairs and a bureau. Maybe she was bidding for buyers who wished to remain secret, but I doubted it. It was time for her to buy that new van, or build on a wing to her house which, visualizing it, I think she had already done, maybe twice.

"Shall we meet again?" she asked, giving me a hug goodbye that warmed me through and through. "I'd like to."

"Definitely," I replied gallantly, but didn't think so. "I'll call." I leaned down and gave her a kiss, not caring who saw, showing my appreciation. "Do you need help loading your stuff?"

"No thanks. Stay here. Your flamingoes are coming up soon." She flexed her arms and damned if her biceps didn't bump up. "What looks like chub is really relaxed muscle. I'm strong as an ox. I'm like one of those Sumo wrestlers. Don't be deceived."

"I'm not deceived. I'm scared."

She went away smiling.

"Nice lady," said Jack, sidling over and taking her seat. "Smart dealer, too. She has a good eye. Have you seen her teddy bear collection?"

I looked at him askance. Was he trying to ascertain if I'd slept with her? Had *he* seen her teddy bear collection?

"Why do you ask?"

"An example. It's worth a quarter of a million."

"Teddy bears? What are they, mink-furred?"

"Look sharp, guy. Here come your birds."

Now I had a problem. My plan was not to bid on the birds but to ascertain who bought them and steal them later. Or steal one of them later. I didn't really need two. I didn't even need one, but no sense in going into those murky waters.

Here I was all worried about Betsy's buying and hoarding compulsion when it was small potatoes compared to my obsessive flamingo filching. Or big potatoes since I stole worthless items and she bought stuff that appreciated in value. (But who would have thought teddy bears?) I decided that, no matter what, this would be my last flamingo. I had told myself ten. This, counting the free one, and counting the Steins' set as two, would fulfill the amount.

The bidding was lively at the outset. I was bothered by being next to Jack, who since I'd shown an interest in the birds, enough to heft one, would be expecting me to bid. He had referred to them as 'my birds'. I didn't want to be noticed and be remembered later, after its theft, as one of the people who bid for the birds at the auction. But I was afraid that, if I didn't bid, it would look suspicious to Jack, as if the reason I wasn't bidding was to prove to him that I didn't care about flamingoes enough to have been his flamingo thief.

Then damned if he didn't lift his paddle. The bidding was now up to six hundred and fifty dollars for the pair. He, who had nothing in his store worth more than twenty cents, was bidding an outrageous price for *my* lawn ornaments.

Was he trying to raise the sum to screw me, or was he actually trying to take them away from me to screw me? Either way, it was an antagonistic act. He had probably decided it was possible for me to be both the Juice

King and the flamingo thief (ie: a faster runner), seeing that one did not cancel the other.

A minute ago I had worried that he would wonder why I wasn't bidding for my birds; now I was upset that he wasn't wondering, didn't care, was blithely bidding for my birds for himself. I felt hurt. Go figure, but I did.

In my life I've always been my own boss and have chosen people to work for me that I like, just as I've chosen friends I like. I think my employees and friends like me in return. So I haven't really had an experience with someone who didn't like me – not counting Stella, since periodically wives are given to hating their husbands and vice versa, but that passes.

In a way, I found Jack's antagonism bracing, but I also had no idea how to handle it. Except for Stella with whom, according to Laurie, I had become meek and milquetoasty, I'd had no experience with hostility.

I had to remind myself that he had every right to feel hostile toward me since I had stolen from his store and run him ragged through his hometown. I had to remember I was no longer a good guy and look at myself anew. I was a lowdown thief who stole from family, friends, cripples, churches, and others much poorer than myself. I was a Grade A creep.

Then it occurred to me that Jack could be bidding for me, thinking I was hamstrung and unable to lift my paddle, thinking I was a pathetic, tyro bidder, unable to do my job.

"I hope you are not bidding for me?"

"Why would I do that?"

"Do you want them yourself?"

"What do you think I'm doing here? Paddling an imaginary canoe?"

I fervently hoped he would fall out of the bidding. I did not want to steal again from Jack. I could raise the bidding out of his purview, as he was perhaps trying to do to me, but it was too chancy. Even standing next to Jack right now was drawing too much attention to me. "See you." I moved off. "Good luck."

From the back of the tent, I checked out the other bidders. The most intrepid seemed to be a hunched, bald, little man who looked like a Dickensian accountant, one who had spent his life on a high stool, bent over volumes of forgotten lore, manhandling numbers, way before the calculator or even the abacus.

I absolutely did not want to steal from a hunchback.

But the bang of the hammer soon convinced me that such was to be the case.

XII

FILCHING THE FINAL FLAMINGO

On closer inspection, I don't think he was an actual hunchback, which comes from a disease called scoliosis and can be controlled these days, in America at any rate, and which twists the spine sideways. One hardly ever sees true hunchbackism any more. This man probably suffered from osteoporosis, more prevalent in older women than men, which causes the spine to bend, dropping the neck so your chin hits your chest. It is also, unlike scoliosis, painful as hell.

I scrunched down in my car, munching a hot dog while watching him load the flamingoes into his van or, rather, direct the loading. There was a young boy with him who did the grunt work. He looked like Jimmy Barnes but how could it be? It's always hard to identify someone so out of context. The hunchback, (as I'll call him since osteoporosis-guy is awkward and I didn't want him to be in pain), was yelling at the boy to load the birds forthwith. It cheered me up that he had a nasty temperament. I could feel better about stealing from him. As long as it wasn't pain making him nasty, then I'd feel worse (see above).

The boy (Jimmy?) did what was required ably and with good spirit, but the old man railed at him as if he were an oaf, causing the boy's cheeks to burn. Soon the van doors slammed shut as the two of them got in and drove off, my Boxster hard on their van's ass.

I kept cars between us all the way to the town of Sonoma which I thought would be his destination, but he turned left on route 12, heading for Glen Ellen, the Valley of the Moon, Jack London's old hideout, if you can call a mansion a hideout, and once there he, the old man not Jack London, kept going, past other, little, one-horse towns like Kenwood and

Oakmont. I say he, but Jimmy did the driving. By now I was sure it was Jimmy.

The thin road snaked through the valley. The green of watered vineyards gleamed next to the dusty, lavender-gold fields of indigenous grasses while the hills displayed the darker green of Oak trees. Bright roses fenced in the vineyards and huge, pink and white oleander bushes kept the dust of the road from private homes and ranches. I had no idea where we were going until we made a right turn up a winding mountain road. This road would take us to the next valley over, the Napa Valley, and the town of Calistoga, a town set at the end of the world famous wine-producing valley.

At this juncture, in the pottering car chase, there were just the two of us on the road, and it could begin to look obvious that I was following him. I should either hang back out of sight or go ahead as the typical Porsche driver would do. He would not hang behind a lumbering van on a kickass, winding, mountain road, but instead would honk the van driver over to a pull-out so he could obnoxiously burn rubber and pass. This was strictly sports car terrain and on such a landscape no crummy van driver gets in our way.

So I moved up on them and Jimmy considerately pulled over for me to pass. I covered the side of my face as I went by and roared ahead five miles to where the road entered Calistoga. Here I tucked into some trees to wait and get an idea where in the town he lived. Naturally I couldn't follow him to his door, but it was a small town and I only needed to know the general neighborhood where later I could go looking for his van. The good thing about this part of the world was that almost nobody parked in their garages, which metamorphosed into family rooms or workshops.

But he didn't drive into Calistoga, he turned right toward St. Helena. What the hell, I thought. We are driving in a huge circle. If the hunchback lived in St. Helena, (which was dubious since there were no ugly, old people there, only winesters and movie stars), he should have taken route 12 from Sonoma to Napa Valley's 29, although he could cannily have intended to avoid the crush of wine-country-tourist traffic by going this circuitous route. More likely he wanted to make the drive an ordeal for his boy helper.

Too bad, though, for me because whereas Calistoga was a hokey, little, western town, slightly known for its geyser, hot springs, mud baths, and landing field where one could rent a glider by the hour, St. Helena was richville. The hunchback could live in a walled and moated mansion where he wouldn't be parking his van on the street to enable me to easily identify his abode.

But he fooled me again. Just before St. Helena he turned left on Deer Park Road and headed uphill to a town called Angwin. There was no reason for me to know anything about this obscure, hill town except that in my road running days I'd run a 10K race there three years in a row, so I knew that the whole town consisted of Seventh Day Adventists and therefore was a dry town, tough on a runner who likes a cold brewski after the race. The Adventists had a school and college of their religious persuasion and, down the road toward richville, a hospital that served the valley. It was the only race where a prayer was said before the starting gun and a moment of silence requested. This was hard on us high-strung runners who had to stop talking about our injuries and how untrained we were, supposedly psyching out the competition thereby, and be quiet for a full sixty seconds. Although the van turned off to Angwin, I had to keep going to St. Helena or my cover would be hopelessly blown. Towns didn't come any smaller than Angwin. I could easily find him. The only flaw in my reasoning would be if he was headed for Pope Valley, where the Angwin road ended, but there were only a few ranchers out there who assuredly wouldn't be seen dead with pink flamingoes. Although, come to think of it, there was a hubcap collector who hung his hoard, hundreds strong, on a fence by the road where they glittered brilliantly in the sun for passers-by to admire. That would be all five passers-by, four of whom were neighbors.

I was hot and tired and sulky, feeling out-puppied by the hunchback. I no longer had a plan. I had to refresh myself. There were lots of good restaurants in St. Helena but I wasn't dressed well enough. I could pass except that my clothes were wrinkled and, where my back met the seat, soaking wet. So, instead, I went into Ana's Cantina, a favorite of the Mexican population. I sat down at the bar and ordered a margarita, which came cold and frothy in a big glass like they served milkshakes in when I was a kid in Maine. Real Mexicans don't use glasses with stems.

The place was full of vineyard workers with a splattering of oenologists such as vineyard managers, wine makers, and possibly even vineyard owners. Everyone dressed down and pretty much alike since the Mexicans bought the others cast-offs at the church rummage sales. Some of the Mexicans wore straw cowboy hats and mustaches to distinguish themselves although their brown skin and small stature already did the trick.

It was six thirty and I was an hour and a half from home. I should call Stella and tell her I wouldn't be home for dinner. What a long day it had been. It seemed like two days ago that I had cleaned the houseboat. Then I had that disturbing talk with Laurie. The awful auction, brightened only by Betsy, also seemed long, long ago.

Pondering my day took me through the first margarita and I ordered a second to drink while making a plan for the finish of the day. I ordered chicken burrito and called Stella who wasn't home. I left a message that I wasn't home either. Returning to my seat, I found Jimmy Barnes on the next stool. "Hello Mr. Forester, er, Tim. I thought that was you in the Boxster behind us, then I just saw your car outside on my way home so ..."

Should I say I had recognized him in the van? Seen him at the auction? It certainly would be awkward if it were his father I was going to steal from. It already was awkward to have followed them. "Hi, Jimmy. This is a nice surprise. What will you have?"

"A beer would be great."

Sure it would be great if he were twenty-one. He was probably seventeen but looked younger, maybe because of being half Asian. Only his nose gave away some Caucasian blood but his eyes had the epicanthic fold, the feathered brows. His hair was black and straight. His skin was smooth with hardly any beard. At the same time he had a tough look about him when he wasn't smiling and when he did smile his face didn't wholly open up. He didn't look boyish.

I ordered a draft from the beefy bartender. Behind him someone had painted a mural of one of Diego Rivera's wife's paintings, an artist Stella loved. I couldn't remember her name, but in this picture (they were always of her own grim self) she held a brightly plumaged bird, not a flamingo. It was a horrible painting. All hers were. Ana's Cantina used to have a terrific mural of a desert scene with a red pick-up truck parked by a dry creek under a blaring sunset sky. Now this. Ana's had gone pretentious. Freda Kahlo, that's who she was.

"I saw you at the auction," Jimmy said, quaffing down half the beer.

I was on ticklish ground. I could pump him for all he was worth about the horrible hunchback's flamingo destination and he would be forthcoming since, one might say, he owed me big time. However he could well have seen me flagrantly nab his mother's flamingo toothpick holder and put two and two together.

"What are you doing in this neck of the woods?"

"Staying with my dad."

"Was that him in the van?"

"No way! Mr. Angley teaches at Pacific Union where my dad teaches. He paid me to help him out today. It wasn't worth it. In the end, he stiffed me, only paid half of what he promised. He's such a creep! Thanks for the beer, Tim."

He was definitely relishing it. "Help yourself to a burrito, too."

"Thanks." He grabbed it like a starving man. I ordered some more.

Too bad Angley was a teacher. That would mean he was off for the summer and would be home during the day. "I bet he teaches French," I said. "I never met a nice French teacher. They are generally hated."

"He's probably the custodian and just says he teaches."

"So ... did he put that pair of flamingoes on his lawn?"

"No, took them indoors. He wouldn't let me come in. Not that I wanted to. It's probably one of those houses that haven't been cleaned in years. Yuk!"

It sent a pang through my heart for poor Stella. If I left her, who would clean her living space? And if nobody did, who would ever want to visit her?

Was I thinking of leaving her?

Stella was not the issue now. My mind scrambled for purchase and came up with an idea. "This Angley character stiffed me, too. He was supposed to be bidding on the flamingoes for both of us — one for me, one for him. Then he took off with both of them. Remember the rush he was in to get away?"

"Yeah." It was a dubious yeah. Jimmy was being polite but he distrusted my story. It was a weak story. For instance, if I had known Angley, wouldn't I have known he wasn't Jimmy's dad? And, if we had made such a deal, why hadn't I simply come over to him at the auction and claimed my flamingo? Oh well.

"I didn't want to cause a scene so I followed him." I was talking a little thickly. The margaritas packed a wallop – the trouble with quart-sized cocktails. Damn Mexicans! Undeterred, my tongue struggled on while my brain tried to keep to simple sentences. "What it comes down to is, he has stolen my flamingo."

"Right on. Let's get it back."

"Jimmy. I need your help."

"Okay!" He sat up straight to show his readiness for action, lifted his chin. Good boy. But I was not a good man to make him my accomplice. I felt like that vile Dickens character, the one who gets young boys drunk and makes them steal for him. I forget his name, not Freda Kahloo although I think it does begin with the letter F, like everything else that's unimportant. Fagin!"

Because of the price of the flamingoes that the hammer knocked down, twelve hundred dollars, I was moving from petty theft to grand theft which carried a prison term for me and Jimmy, but Jimmy would be okay since he now partially believed the flamingo was rightfully mine, and by securing it for me he was not doing anything unlawful.

We attacked the second order of burritos, mouth flamers.

"We've got to get Angley out of his house."

102

"No problem. He's not there now," Jimmy said.

"No?"

"No. I told Dad to ask him over for a drink and get him to fork over the rest of the payment for my work. It wasn't fair. I spent the whole day with Angley – pretty much height of misery. Dad told me to take off and he'd see what he could do."

"Let's go, then. Have you got a car?"

"My dad's. Plenty of room."

It was a Ford Taurus. We hared off to Angwin, first making a pass by Jimmy's father's house where we saw the two men in the illuminated living room. "They're playing gin rummy so there's lots of time." We drove on to Angley's house, two blocks away, a small, beige bungalow with no lawn for lawn ornaments except for a strip of green between the cement path and the cement driveway. There were no flowers but one excellent grapefruit tree stood stolidly by the door, like a yellow and green guard. The shades were pulled over the windows.

"Keep the engine running. This is going to be a quick snatch."

I trotted up the front path. Lights came on, sensing my propinquity, spotlighting me as I picked up a rock by the tree and smashed the long, narrow window at the side of the door. The lights were so bright, I felt like they were attended by band music. I reached in and turned the knob to open the door.

Stepping inside, I stood astounded. The room, first of all, was perfectly clean. It was sparsely furnished because it was crammed full of animal statues: dogs, cats, a zebra, camel, tiger, and elephant. It was like being back in Joy's dollhouse, peopled with animals, only this was all on a human scale. It wasn't entirely on an animal scale. Just as some of Joy's china animals weren't properly scaled to species, so here the elephant was smaller than the tiger, the cockatoo bigger than the dog, but they were all between two and six feet tall. These bright shiny creatures sitting around a living room, on the furniture as well as on the floor, was the most bizarre thing I'd ever seen and strangely enchanting. It made me kind of love the terrible Mr. Angley for having this surprising side to him.

But no time to stand astounded. No time, either, to do as I yearned to and look into the other rooms. I dithered for a minute over which flamingo to choose, decided on 'head up', made the grab, and trundled it back to the car, leaving the house in darkness as before.

Jimmy drove down the hill and we stashed the flamingo in some bushes on the outskirts of St. Helena so I wouldn't be seen with it on the main street when I changed cars. I would get my car and return for it. Although mustn't Jimmy have wondered why, if it was truly my bird, being seen with it would matter?

When he dropped me back in front of Ana's Cantina, he got out of the car. "Thanks for the dinner, Tim. It was fun. And, don't worry. This is our secret." Then, awkwardly, he hugged me.

His young boy's body against mine felt so dear to me. I didn't want to let him go. Jamie would be fourteen now. Fourteen! I could almost be hugging Jamie. I turned quickly to my car so Jimmy wouldn't see my flash flood of tears.

PART TWO — FLAMINGO RETURNS

XIII

FIDELITY

It was around midnight when I got back to the houseboat after dropping Final, as I'd named my last flamingo, at Jamie's house. The huge bird had barely fit in the car. I put the back of the passenger seat down so I could prostrate it and then raised the top of the car so it wouldn't be seen. Ensconced in the bare living room of the Mill Valley house, it took ownership. It was an arrogant-looking bird, a flamingo statesman, not just because of his size, because of the look in his eye, the slant of his beak. It would be nothing for this bird to draw water into his beak and force it out again twenty times a second. Tongue Master.

When I arrived at the houseboat door, I heard footsteps on the dock and stepped back out on the gangplank to see Stella, walking arm in arm with a strange man. I hesitated then hailed her. "Stella!"

She stopped, bid farewell to her escort then came on alone. "Were you looking for me?" she asked.

She smelled strongly of wine. I unlocked the door and she went in ahead walking loosely, but not quite staggering. Maybe the man, whoever he was, was helping her up the dock because of her condition. I turned on the lights. When she looked around at me, she was smiling. "I got your message. What were you doing up in the Napa Valley?"

"Driving. I did the two-valley loop, Sonoma and Napa. I lunched in Petaluma and dined in St. Helena. I went through Calistoga. Notice it all ends with A. It's a California thing."

"Something to do with the Spanish missionaries no doubt." She flopped into an armchair, still smiling. "I'm so happy." Her words flowed out. "I know I shouldn't be, but everything is going so wonderfully at last.

106

Everything I've always dreamed of. You can't understand because you have been a success since early on, but for me it's been work, work, work, and getting nowhere. Years and years sending out slides to galleries and being rejected. Finally I get a show in Mill Valley, a small town, but a goodish gallery, good enough for me, and damned if it doesn't catapult me to success — critically and sales-wise. Now I've got a San Francisco gallery. I've got newspapers interviewing me and, face it, men vying for my charms. Nothing is as sexy as success. I'm sure you've found that to be the case. Women swarm you at parties."

I poured myself an ice water from the spout on the fridge. Outside the view window, a few houseboat lights from across the lagoon glittered in air and water. "I'm glad for you, Stella. I want you to be happy. Don't feel bad that you are. You deserve it. Every bit of it."

"Oh, don't be so fucking nice. Don't patronize me." She tried to sit up straight, but fell back in the chair.

"I'm not."

"Yes you are."

"Then I'm sorry."

"The fact is, the horrible gruesome fact is I feel like I made a pact with the devil. You can have my son, I told him, if I can finally have what I've dreamed of all my life. It's a deal, he said." She waited. "No comment? Nothing nice to say about that? What if it is true? I ask myself, if I could have made such a deal, would I have? Did I? Maybe the answer is yes. Maybe being a mother held me back, took time and energy from my creativity. Maybe, deep down, I wanted to be free."

"I would have stopped working if you had asked me." My voice was trembling. I cleared my throat, as if it were that simple to stop the tremble, as if it were just a breadcrumb lodged there.

"Would you have given up Zeus Juice?"

"Yes."

"Easy to say now when you've lost it anyway."

So she knew.

It was stupid to try to have a discussion with her while she was drunk, but I tried. "And it is easy for you to say I wouldn't have given Zeus up when you didn't ask me then. I think I would have felt it was your turn. We had money enough and Zeus was no longer what it was. It had become a monster."

I talked on about it, anxious to get off the subject of the devil's pact, wandering around the room as I spoke, looking out at the lights, stars, and the darkness where the mountain removed the sky. When I turned to face Stella again, she had fallen asleep. Her shiny hair covered half her face and she looked unfamiliar. She looked old. I left her there and went downstairs.

In bed, when I tried to talk to my son, I was too exhausted. "What can I say, James? It's been a long, crazy day. The only good part was hugging you, I mean thinking I was hugging you. I love you. Good night."

The next morning, Sunday, when Stella got up, I gave her breakfast and was gentle with her. I didn't know if she remembered what she had said the night before. While she ate, I went to water my blimeys and was frightened to see them almost withered. I must be neglecting them. It had been unusually hot. I stood on the deck, putting a fine spray on the leaves and fruit before watering them deeply. Of course, it was possible they hadn't liked the Just So story the other night, were into the more mature Kipling, although I thought his kid stuff was brilliant. I had complained once to Captain Rick that my blimey's couldn't hear the Kipling from his deck so we alternated decks for the reading every blimey night, even though Rick assured me blimeys had hearing like dogs.

"Please revive," I begged.

"Do you feel like taking out the kayaks?" I asked Stella afterward.

"Sure."

The water was calm as a mirror. We slipped over it. The sun caressed us. We headed out into the bay toward Angel Island. Here the water was rougher, then too rough, even tempestuous, although the day was clear. Sometimes waves seem to have their own weather instructions from the deep. It was too dangerous to be out in them. The waves would hide us from the bigger boats. We turned and headed back. When we were side by side in calmer water, passing Clipper Yacht harbor, she said. "That guy you saw me with on the dock last night is my lover. His name is Derek. We've been together a couple of months."

I wasn't surprised. All the cues were there and I think I knew for sure yesterday morning when she had blushed. Still, my heart sank. My arms ceased paddling and, un-noticing, she pulled ahead. When I caught up to her she was still talking about Derek as if sharing her happiness with a friend, forgetting entirely, or so it seemed, that she was addressing her husband.

"He's twenty nine, a yacht broker and, of course, a sailor, too. His office is at the yacht harbor not so far from my studio so we kept running into each other. We ..."

I interrupted. "Are you going to leave me, Stella?"

"No. Good heavens, no." She looked and sounded as if the idea had not entered her mind. Then she added, thoughtfully, "Not at this point at any rate." Going from thoughtful to blithe, she asked, as if we'd long ago agreed on an open marriage, "Any one in your life?"

"Not really."

I paddled ahead of her, sick at heart. I had told myself I wanted her to be happy, that I didn't care if she had ten lovers, and I meant it, but there seemed to be a subtext to all this. I felt an animosity from Stella, as if she were showing me, as if she were getting back at me for something. What had I done? Besides lose my job, that is. She didn't know about the orgy or Betsy or my aberrant flamingo behavior, and there was no point in telling her since it was meaningless. At least I couldn't see any meaning in it. And it was all finished now, with Final. No more thefts.

I wondered if she was angry with me because I was still grieving for Jamie and she wasn't. That being so, was I a constant reprimand to her even though I kept telling her I wanted her to recover? The last stage in the five or seven fucking stages of grief was acceptance. She had reached it. I would never reach it. Jamie's death would always be unacceptable.

Waves of nausea were hitting me. I paddled quickly ahead so that if I vomited she wouldn't see. The boat skimmed over the water. The paddle whirled in my hands. The exercise made me feel better. I was getting an endorphin high, subduing the sickness. Stella and I would get over this. We'd been together nineteen years.

Then I thought some more and wondered if she was as well and happy as she imagined. Mustn't the state of her room be manifesting inner turmoil? She had been messy before, but never so wretchedly filthy. And she was drinking a lot. No matter what, I had to keep looking out for her. I hoped this Derek was a good guy. Maybe I should check him out, talk with him about Stella.

When I got home I went to work moving my desk, chair, and filing cabinets into my bedroom. It was a tight fit, but now Joy could have a room that was completely her own when she came to visit. The pillow concoction didn't work that well as a bed and Stella would want them back. I seemed to remember that Betsy had some antique beds for children in her shop, one called a Snow White bed, light green with hand-painted flowers on it. And she had pretty quilts, too. Not to mention teddy bears. Tomorrow I would go by and make some purchases. I returned the pillows to Stella's room, then returned to Joy's room to move out the plant, the rug, all the little things Joy had put in, so I could vacuum. Afterward I took a wet cloth to the woodwork. She would need proper curtains, too.

Meanwhile, Stella had still not returned – probably she'd made a stop at the yacht harbor to tell Derek she'd told me about the two of them. I headed over to Mill Valley to see George, Laurie, and Joy. It would cheer me up.

When I got to the door of their house, I could see through the etched glass window into the living room where a couple was embracing. When I rang the doorbell, they detached. One came to the door and let me in. It was the nanny, her face warm and flushed.

Everything was falling apart. I told myself to turn and go, but my feet took me into the living room. When I entered, George was not there. The other half of the embracing couple was Laurie, not George. Laurie!

The nanny went on to the kitchen and Laurie, seeing my face, came right over to me, drew me to the couch and sat beside me. "You saw?"

I opened my mouth to speak, but nothing came. I nodded miserably.

"It's okay, Tim. It's nothing. Gay women are always falling in love with me, but I'm not inclined that way. I was just comforting her. I suppose I should give it a try sometime, but the fact is, I'm not a sexy person, with men or women. I'm too wholesome. I like hugs. I like warmth. But sex? I've never understood what all the fuss is about."

I was reassured. It helped me understand George's sexual behavior, too … somewhat. I told Laurie about Joy's room which she had already heard some about yesterday. "Is it okay if I go ahead and fix it up so it is her own little room and then she can spend the night sometime, if she wants to, maybe when she is a little older. Or she could just have a nap there. Or play."

"Of course! Joy loves the houseboat. And I'd much rather leave her with you than baby sitters when I'm off playing golf. Our nanny will be leaving us in the fall, but what about your life, Tim? What are you going to do now that you've left Zeus?"

"How about, in the fall, I become Joy's nanny?"

"If you are serious about that, I could even go back to work, help out George. There's no one I'd trust more to look after Joy than you. And this year she'll be old enough for play school so it wouldn't be an all-day job." She added, rather dolefully, "I've been offered a job in the D.A.'s office."

"Laurie, why don't you see how far you can go with your golf? Otherwise you'll always wonder. I know George would be behind you all the way. There's money enough and I'll nanny Joy for free, of course."

She threw herself into my arms. "You angel!"

Holding her in my arms, I said, "You seem pretty sexy to me. But I've always found happiness sexy."

George and Joy arrived home from a hike with the Steins and with Flintstone who threw himself down on the rug exhausted. He was not a mountain dog. Give him a bull or burglar to chase and he'd show his stuff, but trails were not his terrain, too many rocks and roots, too much up and down. A pasture was good. A floor was best.

We all made merry the rest of the day and evening, George not firing up the barbecue so as not to tangle with Alvin, but making a hearty Maine beef stew to simmer away in the oven while we drank a pitcher of margaritas, produced by Alvin, Alvin commenting on their proper coldness. Maybe his need to control only had to do with temperatures and so Marie let him be. He'd probably be hell to have around an air conditioner.

I didn't call Stella and it didn't seem to occur to anyone to suggest that I urge her to join us.

I told Joy that when her current nanny left, I was going to be her nanny and she asked, worriedly, "Can you be a uncle and a nanny, too?"

"You bet."

A phrase came back to me from my church-going days as a kid, *The Lord giveth and the Lord taketh away.*

I told Marie how it had jumped into my mind, since it was part of her area of expertise. "Yes," she said. "And the wonderful thing is that although He sometimes does most cruelly take away, He never stops giving. Abundantly. It's just that sometimes we don't notice."

XIV

FEAR

The next day at Betsy's shop, I bought the Snow White bed for Joy along with a pink and yellow quilt, a blue bedside table. "And I have just the thing to go on the bedside table," Betsy said, revealing one of the perfect, little Art Deco radios that I had seen at the Petaluma auction, jade green, shaped like a prostrated apostrophe. "A present from me to you."

"I can't accept this. The broken flamingo was one thing but this is major money."

"I saw how you loved it. I like people to own old things who love them. The people who buy these are collectors hoping to make a buck on them. You can play this one, too. Most of them don't work. I've had it for years and didn't pay much at the time of purchase."

"Thank you, Betsy. I'm very touched." I tried to think of the last time Stella bought me a present and nothing came to mind – but that was mean thinking, not allowed.

"Speaking of old flamingoes," Betsy said, "I talked to Jack this morning. He gets the Santa Rosa paper and there was an article in there about the flamingoes from the auction. One of them was stolen from the guy who bought them. Jack is naturally wondering if it was the same flamingo thief."

"How come you talk to Jack so much?"

Betsy flushed. "He's my husband."

"No."

"Yes."

"But your shop is so bright, beautiful, and tasteful. His is hideous."

Betsy was quiet. I realized that now she knew I'd been to his shop. Oops! It wasn't proof that I was the flamingo thief but it was close. Very close.

I could see her mind working. She was not permitting herself to think that I was anything but an ex-juice-king and nice new friend.

"He makes a fortune at that shop," she said, defensively, but also teaching me. "He keeps it looking that way on purpose so that the tourists will think they really made a find from a guy who doesn't know what he's selling. What he has is a lot of collectibles that people look high and low for, things like old wrenches, fountain pens, lunch boxes, costume jewelry, and he doesn't ask much for them." She sighed. "The reason they are cheap is because most of them are copies made to look old which he has actually created for the shop. This is not unusual in the business, but I, myself, condemn the practice. It's partly why we separated, although I still love him. I learned a lot about antiques from him,"

"He told me you have a good eye."

Surprisingly, she blushed with pleasure. "That's high praise from Jack."

"Tell me what the article said about the stolen flamingo."

"His name is Angley and it was stolen from his house in Angwin. He said he was determined to recover it because, and this was quite cute, he said the pair was inseparable."

Angley and cute were a contradiction in terms, an oxymoron.

I dropped the subject, saying, "I'll need to have the bed delivered."

"Okay, help me put it in the van. Of course we'll have to take some things out first. Then we'll go to my house on the way. I've made some changes I want to show you."

115

We went to her house. She still had to leave a breadcrumb trail for me to find the way to the bedroom but once there I found it transformed. The stuffed animals had gone to teddy bear heaven and the rest of the room was stripped down to bureau, dressing table, and chair (all from the auction) bed, bedside tables with lamps, and a cozy, slip covered armchair with a footstool. A hooked rug, of birds in a garden, lay on the shiny floor, and long, filmy curtains hung by the windows.

It was charming, a great place to spend the afternoon, which we did. I felt much more comfortable with her this time. She didn't take me to the heights I experienced with Stella but it was nice and I was grateful.

At the end of the day, in the garden, I told her about Jamie. "He was a wonderful kid, so happy all the time, so good-natured. There wasn't anything special about him. He wasn't particularly smart, wasn't musical, or even athletic, but he was full of love and laughter, full of life. I swear he liked everybody. I'm sure I must misremember and glorify him, but I can't recall him ever complaining about anything or sulking or hitting a kid younger than him."

Betsy refilled my wine glass with a tasty sauvignon blanc. She listened calmly. She was easy to talk to.

"He even ate all his food at meals and said thank you to his mom and me at the end, like he was grateful he had good providers. He never asked for stuff the way kids always do, wanting the latest fad in clothes or gear. He didn't care what he wore, what he had or hadn't."

Betsy nodded.

"He loved creatures. His room was full of cages of animals and reptiles, which he had bought or caught. He tended to them lovingly and carefully. At an early age he became a vegetarian because he just couldn't see eating something whose heart beat."

I sipped the wine, taking it slow after two nights of margaritas.

"That was the only thing in which he and I differed. I couldn't give up real food. To me a meal without meat isn't a meal. He was deeply disappointed that I wouldn't go along with him but he forgave me when he was around eight. His mom did become a vegetarian and still is. But the thing I want to describe is that Jamie and I were pals. We'd rather be together than with anyone else. I feel like half a person now, the worst half."

It was only later, having an early supper together in the patio of a local restaurant, that Betsy told me she had lost three babies trying to bring them to term. "I'm not telling you this to compare my grief in any way with the grief you feel because I never even got to hold those children in my arms, let alone share a life with them, but just so you'll know I have an idea what you've suffered, and so you'll know that, if we ever did fall in love with each other, I couldn't give you a child, much as I'd want to with all my heart."

"Betsy, if you have lost children and you know you can't have any others, tell me how you go through life with a smile on your face, being so happy."

"What's the alternative, honey? What other way would I possibly want to be? Grumpy and scowling? I don't think so."

"But can you choose to be happy even if you don't feel it?"

"Yes, I think you can because it's such a good choice."

After dinner she followed me to the dock in her van. I piled half the stuff on one of the shopping carts that the dock provided to wheel marketing to the houseboats. As I was doing so, Stella showed up, coming down the dock from the boat, stopping to get the mail out of the rank of mailboxes at the dock entrance.

"What's all this?" she exclaimed.

"Stella, this is Betsy." I gestured toward the nearby van. Betsy, hauling out the side slats for the bed, yelled hello. Stella wore the currently fashionable, retro Capri pants, high wedgie sandals, and a loose, white, tee shirt. Maybe it was from being with Betsy but she looked terribly thin.

"I bought some stuff for Joy's room," I explained, trying not to look hangdog.

"I see." She looked at me with narrowed eyes. When Betsy put the slats in the cart, Stella asked her, "Did Tim tell you we have a little girl named Joy? The fact is, we don't, and all these purchases are utter madness."

Betsy looked from one to the other of us with a small frown between her brows. I had not said anything to her about Joy. Perhaps she did assume we had a daughter. Now, maybe she was thinking that I had an imaginary daughter. I carefully explained. "I have a niece named Joy who comes to stay with us sometimes."

The fact was, she never had stayed with us overnight, but I hoped Stella would say nothing more about it.

"You wish," Stella said. Then, suddenly, she turned sweet, put an arm around me and kissed me. "Poor darling," she said. "Do as you want. I'll see you later. There's a birthday party for Arnold, the egg artist at Liberty Café. Do you want to come?"

"Maybe I'll join you in a little while."

"Nice to meet you, Betsy."

"Nice to meet you, Stella."

"She's beautiful," Betsy said, watching her cross the parking lot and get into her Toyota pickup. Then, turning to me, she added, "But what a bitch."

"I love her," I told Betsy earnestly.

"I know. I can tell."

The next day, five pages into the *San Francisco Chronicle*, there was an article entitled: Angwin's Angley Anguished.

The story read: A Mr. Angley of Angwin has had his plaster flamingo stolen, one of an "inseparable pair". He says the local police are laughable and has hired a private detective. He suspects a man at the auction he saw bidding for the pair of birds, which sold for twelve thousand dollars. "The same man followed me home in a Porsche. No one steals from me and gets away with it. I will track him to the ends of the earth."

My face turned red, reading this completely erroneous article. Obviously the *Chronicle* picked up the item from the Santa Rosa paper because of the irresistible wordplay possibilities. The report was a tissue of lies. Never mind the extra zero they added to the price. The true facts were: I did not bid on the birds. I did not follow him "home."

I felt the same indignation I'd felt when being accused of having held the flamingo "aloft" when stealing from Jack's Alleged Antiques, as if to me the details were more important than the theft itself. I wanted so much for the world to hear my side of Angley's story that it actually occurred to me to write a letter to the editor to straighten out the facts of the case. As well, I was indignant because it made me wonder about all the newspaper stories I read daily, how mistaken most of them probably were, if this one was any indication, when all these years I'd taken them on complete trust.

So I fulminated in my mind, muttering imprecations aloud (luckily Stella had left for her studio) then my mind stopped cold to consider the more important news: that I was in danger from this detestable hunchback. He had hired a detective. He was going to track me to the ends of the earth. (Should ends be plural or was that another reportage error? Does the earth

119

have more than one end? How could it have any end if it were round?) Well, Sausalito was nowhere near any of earth's ends so he would not have to track me far. And there were not that many owners of the new Boxster, if he had noticed the Porsche type. The detective would have an easy time of it, just by calling the Porsche dealers and getting names of purchasers and comparing them to names at the auction, which we all gave when we got our paddles. (Why in hell did I get a paddle?) Plus, Angley had a description of me if he thought I was the bidder simply because I stood beside the bidder (Jack). Unless he thought the Porsche driver was Jack.

I could end up in prison over this stupidity, my already ruined life ruined further. I wouldn't be able to be Joy's nanny. And, when I came out of prison, an old con, a lag, she'd be too grown to need a nanny anymore and certainly not a jailbird nanny.

Now my mind stopped cold again. What about Betsy? She was the only one who could put the "bidder" together with the "Porsche driver". Now she would unquestionably understand that I, and no other, was the scum-of-the-earth flamingo thief.

Then, with a pang, I realized she was not alone. (I was having small seizure upon small seizure.) Jimmy, my partner in crime, would know even better than Betsy that I was the thief. He would know for sure.

I paused to consider why I felt a pang over Jimmy knowing, but not over Betsy. Well, he was a child. He liked me. He had hugged me. Now he would know I had lied to him, that I had used him. I would lose him forever as a friend just when I had found him. I wondered if he was still in Angwin or back home in Mill Valley. Maybe he had just been there for the weekend. I should call him right away and … and say what? I didn't know what to say.

I looked in the phone book, found his number then, miraculously, the phone rang and it was Jimmy Barnes.

"Tim, it's Jimmy."

"Jimmy, I was just about to call you."

"I saw the paper and just want to tell you not to worry. I won't say anything. I know you took the flamingo for fun and because Angley had been such a rat to me. You were helping me get revenge, right?"

Oh, generous-hearted Jimmy!

"I never believed the story about the deal you made with him to share the flamingoes because how would you even know him?"

"Well, right, but ..."

"And I know you had no idea where he lived until I took you there."

"Right." Here was my chance to set the record straight at least with one person. "And I didn't bid on the flamingoes either, but I was there at the auction and he might have noticed me because the guy standing next to me was bidding."

"Then he will describe the other guy to the detective."

Jimmy was discussing the case with gusto. I entered into his spirit. "Good. I hadn't thought of that."

Although, clearly, when the detective found Jack, Jack would send him directly and joyfully to me.

"He won't be able to track you to the ends of the earth." Jimmy laughed.

"Jimmy, did your dad get the money Mr. Angley owed you?"

"You won't believe this. Angley told dad I'd put a dent in his van so he deducted that from my wage. That dent had been there for a million years. What a creep! I think we should take the other flamingo, too."

121

We talked a little longer. I invited him and his brother, Paul, to come kayaking with me today and told him to meet me at Sea Trek, the kayak rental place, at noon. I said goodbye, because someone was bonging the ship's bell by the door. It was George, carrying the *Chronicle*, open to the page.

XV

FLAMINGO ORDER OF RETURN

"George, come in."

"I saw this in the paper ..."

"Coffee?"

"... and I'm thinking, Porsche driver and flamingo nut. Why does that sound like a familiar combination, a unique combination, so I went to Jamie's house where those flamingoes have been accumulating ..."

"The *mat...*"

"Whatever ..."

"Here." I passed him a cup and he followed me to the living room where I sat on the couch putting my cup on the coffee table. He, too, put his cup down, but kept on standing, looking like a cartoon character of an upset person, hair funny, drops of perspiration hanging in the air around his head, hands gesturing blurrily. Or maybe I was seeing him through the eyes of an upset person.

"... and sure enough, there is a new flamingo at the house, a big one, but I'll eat my hat if it's worth half of twelve thousand dollars."

"It's not. Half of twelve hundred. A misprint. Or Angley lying through his teeth. And that's not all ..." I started to go into my article correction routine, but I contained myself. George needed reassurance. His concerns were deeper than how bad the reporter was.

"What is going on, Ears?" He sat down and took a big slurp of coffee. "I haven't said anything about the flamingoes because," he shrugged, "why can't a guy furnish his house with little pink birds if he wants to. It goes along with his having an empty house in the first place. Knowing you,

123

you'll turn it into a million dollar flamingo museum. "But …" he shook his head sadly. "This Angley guy means trouble. What was it, a prank?"

Jimmy had thought it was a prank, too. Maybe it was. "Sort of," I said, an echo of George's 'not really', ringing the changes of vagueness.

"If he finds you, through the car or the auction, the next thing you know you're in prison, although God knows you could plead diminished capacity."

"Why is that?"

"Because you're in grief, remember? You've not only lost your child, but now you've lost your business, which is like another child, and which you're completely in denial about, Marie says."

I didn't tell him I'd lost my wife, too.

"This flamingo theft thing. You're acting out. Although why with flamingoes is anyone's guess."

"Do you think I'm crazy?"

"No, I don't think you're crazy, but, let's say you're not yourself."

Suddenly, maybe because it was all I had left, I remembered the blimeys. I jumped up, rushed out to the deck to see how they were. Okay. They had revived. A few of the leaves were shot, wrinkled and sere from the overheating, but the fruit looked okay. Some of the flower petals had fallen off and wouldn't fruit, each flower worth a thousand dollars toward Captain Rick's older old age, not that he didn't eat them as fast as they ripened, not that I didn't.

"What's the matter?" George joined me on the deck, looking anxious. "Are the blimeys okay?"

"Yeah, but they looked sunk yesterday. I'd hate to lose my blimeys on top of everything else."

"I thought at the time, they didn't like the *Just So Story*. Too silly. They liked it when we read Kim."

"And some of the short stories."

"Definitely not the poetry," we said in unison and laughed.

"Look, George, if anything happens to me, will you look after the blimeys?"

"Cut it out. Nothing's going to happen to you."

"And I want Joy to have the Mill Valley house because, you see, by the time she grows up, no young people will be able to afford to buy houses around here. There will be nothing under a million dollars. They'll have to kill their parents so they can inherit their houses. This way, I'm saving your life."

"I hate this talk. What you've got to do is give the flamingo back. Pronto."

I lit up. It was like a rock being rolled off my shoulders. Great idea. It was so simple. "Yes! Yes, I'll give it back. Brilliant! I'll give them all back." I smiled happily.

"All? Please don't tell me you've stolen all those flamingoes. Well?"

"You said not to tell you."

"Right. I don't want to hear about it. Or think about it. All I'm saying is, get Angley's flamingo back first."

"I can't. I will have to return them in the order than I took them."

George sighed heavily. Familiar with my compulsive nature, he knew it was senseless to argue.

"Don't worry, George beloved, brother most dear."

He finished his coffee. "I'm going to work. Do you think you can get them all back today?"

I considered. The flamingo-territory-of-return was extremely far flung. "No, but I'll start right away. I'll do my best."

A half hour later, I had loaded all the flamingoes but Final from Jamie's house into the Boxster trunk for hasty returning. The order of return was this: Joy's Uno, Arnold's Dagwood, the Steins set of two, the Zeus Juice secretary's mug, the Catholic Church's spoon-holder, Jack's Ugly, Lisa, Paul, and Jimmy's toothpick-holder. Finally Final. Meanwhile Final, posturing away, lorded it over the house alone.

Betsy's gift, the free flamingo, did not need to be returned so there were only nine in the order. But it did seem like a lot. As I closed the trunk on the bevy, I had a weak moment and wished I could jump up and down on the lot of them.

Then I remembered I had asked Paul and Jimmy to kayak with me today at noon. We were going to Angel Island where we would lunch at the café, fool around, maybe hike or rent bikes, then paddle back. This would take two, maybe three precious hours, curtailing any mass return today. The most I could hope for was Uno and Dagwood's return, maybe the Steins' pair.

The time element fired me up about my mission, and the good thing about returning them versus stealing them was that I wouldn't have to wear the cargo pants or the howible red shirt.

I called George on my cell phone but he was in the operating theater. I left a message asking him to invite the Steins over for cocktails this evening because it was crucial to the plan we discussed this morning. I hoped he would understand and act upon my message. Some of his operations went on for eight or ten hours. I had to get into the Steins' house without them there.

First on the agenda was Uno, first and easiest and most pleasurable. Joy was in the front yard as if she were waiting for me. "Let's go play china animals," I said gaily.

"Me waiting for a fwend. *I* waiting."

This was bad news. When one of her friends came over, Uncle Tim was dross.

"Can't we play until she comes?" Joy was the only person I allowed myself to whine with.

"Sowwy, Uncle Tim. Me and I waiting. Where's Jamie?"

"Jamie died."

"I forgot."

"Do you remember him? He had dark, shiny hair like Stella and such a big smile. His eyes sparkled. He used to carry you around. You adored him. We all did."

I so much wanted Joy to remember him now and forever, but she was so little when he was alive. He'd been dead a third as long as her whole life, a long time for her, although fourteen months was nothing for me, only one thirty-eighth of my life. And who of us remember back to when we were two-something? Eventually, soon, she would forget Jamie. She would completely forget him.

"Here comes my fwend." A car door opened. A little girl tumbled out and ran toward Joy while Joy ran to meet her at the gate, transfigured with happiness.

I went into the house, upstairs to Joy's playroom. I put the flamingo in the dollhouse, in the doll bathroom where I had found it almost two months ago. Back then my life had seemed so impossibly sad. Since then, I'd lost my job and my wife and an angry hunchback was after me but I didn't feel any sadder, despairing maybe, but not sadder. In a way, I was coming to an understanding about my life, which was that I was never going to get over losing my son, and therefore, I was no use to anybody ever again. I was a man half here in this world, dispirited, disembodied.

I sat in front of the dollhouse that was a miniature of Angley's. George had said that Marie said I was in denial over losing Zeus Juice. What was there to deny? Smarter men than I had come and seized it, men with blow-dried, gelled hair who tried and failed to dress down to Zeus's casual standards, but who never had owned a pair of faded jeans in their regimented lives. It was undeniable that I didn't care about the company anymore. There was nothing for me to do there, no son to pass it on to. And I had more money than I would ever need even if Stella took half.

Maybe I was resentful that Stella had gone on with her life, worked harder than ever at her art, and opened her heart to a new love. I loved her and wanted her to be happy, but I wanted her to be happy with me. Now I knew she couldn't be happy with me because I was always going to be sad.

I tried to think seriously about why I was, or had been, stealing flamingoes. George said I was not myself that I was acting out, but that didn't mean anything to me. It was not an answer. Possibly I stole them simply to have something to do, something to engage me. I could take it further, go deeper, and say to myself that I stole from people who had what I wanted: a family, a faith, meaningful work, a dog. But it didn't explain my stealing from Jack or Angley or the Zeus secretary. I think it was simply to have something to do and to experience some excitement, a brief sense of being fully alive, not half, and now, thank God, I had something else to do, which was to return them before Angley caught up with me. It wouldn't be as exciting but it would be tricky, exacting. It would engage me.

128

I took the boys kayaking, paddling my single kayak to Sea Trek then renting a double kayak for them. It was too bad I had to keep to the proper order of flamingo return. I could have slipped them the toothpick holder and crossed it off. As it was, it was far down the list, next to last.

We had a great time. First, staying close to shore, I taught them how to paddle and they both picked it up fast. I had them fall out of the kayak and taught them to get back in. Once on Angel Island, we rented mountain bikes and biked around the peripheral road. At lunch in the café, I told them all about how this had been the place immigrants from the Far East checked into America and the turn of the last century, San Francisco's Ellis Island, which they already knew about from school trips, more than I did. They told me how the Chinese had brought plants from home, which were confiscated and the confiscators planted them on the island where some still exotically flourished. We spent a half hour in the museum. We fooled around endlessly, even joining a volley ball game a group of rowdies had set up in the park by the water.

They were good boys. They fought, but brothers are supposed to fight. Jimmy felt he had to keep Paul in line and Paul felt he had to periodically annoy the hell out of Jimmy, but they were both cheerful and outgoing for teens, not sullen and withdrawn as so many seem to be, or seem to want to appear to be, thinking it cool.

During a few minutes alone, while Paul was in the bathroom, I told Jimmy I was going to return Angley's flamingo and he was surprisingly relieved. "I'll help," he said. "Do you want to do it today?"

"Well, I have these other things I have to do first. You see, I'm a compulsive person and I have to do things in a certain order or I feel they won't come out right."

"That's tough," he commiserated.

Was it tough? I supposed it might appear so to others. Maybe even to me if I thought about it.

"So, tomorrow, then?"

He seemed anxious about it. I wanted to promise, but I didn't see how it could be as soon as tomorrow with only Uno returned at this point. One flamingo a day wouldn't cut it. I had to seriously step up the pace.

"I'll call you, Jimmy."

At Sea Trek I said goodbye. Again Jimmy hugged me and Paul gave me an awkward half-hug. I hoped one of them would marry Joy and live in Jamie's house one day, happily ever after. They were such good boys and Joy would need an older man to steady her. When I changed my will so that she inherited Jamie's house, I would put in this desire, that she marry Paul or Jimmy, at least look them up when she was of age, give them a chance at wooing her.

When I got back to the houseboat, it was almost five o'clock and I'd only returned one flamingo. I was determined to knock off Dagwood, my favorite, the only one of the ten I was actually loath to relinquish — Dagwood, so pretty and forlorn, so understanding.

There was a message from George saying the Steins couldn't come until tomorrow. That meant a whole day lost unless I breached the Order of Return, which every cell in my body cried out Not To Do!

I walked down Gate Five Road to the Industrial Center Building and circled it. Dagwood swung from my hand in a drawstring, plastic bag. I wasn't sure how I was going to do this. If Arnold were gone, I could leave the bag at his door, hanging from the doorknob, and be away free, but I would worry about someone else finding and taking it. It would not be a pure return. His studio was on the ground floor. If his window were open, that would be a boon. I could slip Dagwood through it, onto the windowsill where he had previously resided.

The window wasn't open, Arnold was inside, and he saw me peering in. He waved and smiled.

I walked in the door and down the hall to his studio. "I've come to buy an egg," I said, thinking I would give it to Betsy. (Strange that I still hadn't heard Betsy's reaction to the *Chronicle's* take on Angwin's Anguished Asshole. Did she have my cell number?)

I put the bag containing Dagwood on the top of a book shelf, looked over the eggs, and chose one of a red car on a country road which reminded me of the lost, possibly painted-over, mural at Ana's Cantina of the red pickup truck on the desert.

As Arnold packaged the egg for me, he chatted about Stella and her big success. "It gives us all hope," he said. "Not that we're not deep down jealous and hate her for it," he laughed.

We talked a little longer, then I left, but he came wheeling after me with the bag I had set on his shelf. "Your bag," he cried.

I should have had the presence of mind to say it was not my bag, but I didn't. I took it with thanks. Now what? What did I do now, go and buy another egg so as to try to leave the bag again? Who would I give that egg to?

Maybe an attempted flamingo return counted as a real return. I did not think so. Impure As Hell.

I stood in the hallway shilly-shallying.

If I left the bag at his door later, he'd recognize it, the size and heft of it, the fact it was a blue, drawstring, plastic bag with white letters on it.

Just then a kid came skateboarding around the hall corner and crashed into me. I went down and so did Dagwood and the egg. "Sorry, Mister. Are you okay?"

"Sure. Forget it." Dazed, I struggled to a sitting position, not in a big hurry to get all the way up. My butt rang with pain. Here came Arnold – once again wheeling down the hall toward me.

"You little brat, how many times have I told you not to skateboard in these halls?"

"Fuck you, Crip." He jumped on his board and tore away.

"Kids. I hate 'em. Can you get up?" He extended a hand at the end of a muscular arm, which I availed myself of. "Let me see if the egg's okay." He unpacked the bag he'd prepared for me.

I knew Dagwood was not okay. I could tell by the sound of broken piece on broken piece, jingling. It made me want to cry. Dagwood had stood around for more than fifty years in all his pretty pinkness and now, in a sad minute, was forever smashed. I longed to look in the bag to see if he was salvageable, but I could tell by looking at the outside that the Dagwood shape had transmogrified to smithereens, pieces clinging to the bag's bottom, poking sharply through.

Let's see. Did this count as a return? I was new at this return business, but the fact was, I could make my own rules. This had to count as a return, because I was not about to give Arnold this smashed flamingo. No way.

However, as long as it was still in my possession, it wasn't really returned, which would preclude my returning the others of the *mat*.

"Are you sure you're okay," Arnold looked concerned. "The egg survived."

Speechlessly, I handed him the blue bag with the white letters. He loosened the top and looked inside. "My flamingo?"

132

I nodded.

"Fuck."

We looked at each other, not saying anything. I had lost my voice in any case. All the saliva had drained from my mouth as if it were pulling together to form a wave at the back of my throat that would inundate my teeth, toppling them over.

"You were giving it back to me. That's why you bought the egg. As a cover. This is really shitty, man." He looked at me, waiting for me to speak, but I didn't. I still couldn't. "This was my mother's, you know."

I was hoping he wouldn't get into that. I felt small enough. Shrunken. My head felt like a shrunken head, voiceless, with a wave inside.

"Well, what the hell. You were giving it back, right?" He laughed a little bitterly. "But then I gave it back to you. Then it got broken and I guess I'll never know why you gave it back to me broken."

No sense in getting into the Order of Return with him.

"Better I'd never known you took it, right?"

I nodded. How long was he going to go on with this, beating a man when he was down, even though he had helped him up.

"Maybe I can fix it." He put the bag on his lap and wheeled away back to his studio.

Two down.

XVI

FOWLING UP AGAIN

I wasn't worried about Stella discovering the Angley affair because she only read the *New York Times*, a pretension of hers, but the next morning, having breakfast together, an occurrence that had become less and less usual with us, as had lunch and dinner together, she said, folding her paper to the page, "Listen to this: "Angwin"s Anguished Angley Fights Back. Mr Angley, of Angwin California, anguished over his stolen flamingo, one of an inseparable pair, is on the track of the Porsche driver he suspects is the thief. The suspect also bid on the pair at the auction where they were purchased by Angley for twelve thousand dollars. "I heard that high whine a Porsche makes in low gear from the neighbor's house where I was visiting at the time of the theft," Angley said, "and a Porsche followed me home from the auction. Not many in Northern California have this new type Porsche Boxster. I have a detective on it and a trap set if he returns for the second flamingo."

Additional lies. Does a Taurus, the true vehicle I was in, have a high whine? I think not. I defied Angley to find one neighbor who had seen, heard, or even imagined my Boxster anywhere in Angwin ever, my Boxster which, unlike its owner, never whined. At the same time, I couldn't resist asking Stella, "Was it a real flamingo?"

"Of course not." She looked at me speculatively. "A real flamingo at an auction? In a Porsche?"

"It doesn't say it wasn't real," I insisted, trying to interest her in this side of the tale, rather than her more lively interest in the Porsche driver.

"That's not the point. The point is, isn't it strange? Here is another stolen flamingo in our lives."

"Not exactly in our lives. I wouldn't say that. It's simply in the paper."

"I'm not an idiot, Tim. You have the particular car. You were in the Napa Valley three days ago, and flamingoes have been going missing all around you. I don't care about Angley's, but if you took Arnold's I'll never forgive you."

I must have looked hurt because she quickly said, "I don't mean that." She rustled her paper impatiently. "Why don't you get mad at me when I say things like that?" she asked unreasonably. "Why don't you show your feelings?"

"By showing feelings, you seem to mean shouting and being unkind. Why should I act angry if I'm not? Do feelings have to be loud?"

"Fuck feelings. Did you take the flamingo or not?"

I didn't know which flamingo she meant, Arnold's or Angley's. I'd lost track. Not that the answer wasn't the same.

"I mean, why would you?" Looking baffled, she put down the paper and threw up her hands. "The whole thing is nuts. It doesn't make sense. Are you crazy? I really don't want to live with a crazy man. I'm not up to it."

What happened to our vow of for better or for worse, in sickness and in health? Probably she was looking for any reason to leave me so she could constantly be with her yacht broker instead of just half the time. Young Derek. "Bad for your career," I commented with a sneer engendered by thoughts of the broker.

"I know you hate it that I'm a success now while you are on the downslide."

"How can you say something so completely untrue, knowing me as well as you do? It makes me think you are the crazy one," thus entering into the most bootless subject a married couple can discuss – which of them is crazy.

"You are trying to avoid the subject of these flamingoes."

"If I stole these flamingoes, where are they? Especially Angley's, which is five feet tall!" Haughtily I walked out of the boat to prevent further discussion, leaving her to search my room, and probably Joy's room, too, the adorable room of which Joy had not yet taken possession, but would when I was her nanny, if I wasn't in jail.

Stella followed me out and shouted at me from the gangplank, "How do you know it is five feet tall?" Surely she was puzzling the other docksters. There were always docksters hanging out on the dock: watering plants, chatting together, or just being nosey. Dock life was like a giant, elongated, open-air, college dormitory. Sometimes it took me fifteen minutes to walk the dock to the parking lot because of all the people to pass the time of day with en route.

One neighbor called after me, "Know what is five feet tall?"

"A flamingo."

"I knew that."

"That sounds about right," said another.

Meanwhile there had come another message from George saying the Steins wanted to have cocktails at their house with all of us. He didn't get the picture that I'd stolen flamingoes from them and needed their house empty to return them. But in any case, I determined to make the Stein return this morning and so be able to go on to the next in the Order, which would be the mug belonging to the secretary at Zeus Juice.

It was a warm, breezy day. A summer fog foamed over the ridge that separated us from the Pacific, but then disappeared into the blue. I drove to the Steins' hillside home and scouted around the place. I saw Alvin leave the house with Flintstone, taking him for a walk. This was good. Marie had said Alvin never walked Flintstone so it must mean she was not at home, ergo he had to walk him. The coast was clear.

I went to the trusty bathroom window, but this time it was locked. I would have to break in and the quicker the better. I picked up a rock as I had done at Angley's then smashed the pane. I reached in and unlocked the window, raised it up and threw myself into the opening – head, arms and shoulders first. The creamer was in one jean front pocket, the sugar bowl in the other.

Then everything happened very fast. Marie entered the bathroom with a gun, which she promptly shot without even the accustomed, cautionary, 'Hands Up', which would not have been possible in any case since my hands were reaching for the floor to support my entering body. Nor would, 'Don't Move or I'll Shoot' do the job since my body was in flight. Anyhow, she dispensed with warnings entirely and shot the gun.

Since I was in plunging motion at the time, the bullet hit my arm just below the shoulder, rather than my head. I continued the fall into the bathroom, but this time, as I couldn't catch myself with my hands because of being wounded, I fell in a heap at her feet, cracking my head against the column of the sink. I heard her say, "Tim? Is it you?" then all, even the white porcelain, went black.

When I came to, she and Alvin were fighting.

"I heard the shot. What in hell?"

"Just help me get him on the couch. It's a flesh wound. Don't call 911. A bullet wound automatically will involve the police. It's too embarrassing for us all."

"You shot Tim Forester. Why? Was it a lover's quarrel? How long has he been in the house? How long has this been going on?"

"Please boil some water."

"Why should I? Let him bleed to death, the son of a bitch."

"Alvin, Tim is not my lover. Although I've often wished he were."

My ears pricked up at that. I had no idea Marie was hot for me. I would look at her with new eyes, when and if I ever opened the old ones.

"So, what is he doing here?"

"I have no idea. He came through the bathroom window."

"Oh sure." His voice was heavy with scorn.

The flamingoes, needless to say, were broken in each pocket. Probably I was bleeding from each groin as well as from my arm and head, all four of which really hurt.

Marie left me to boil the water herself. Alvin went to the phone to, of all things, call Stella. He told her with a certain amount of zest that Marie had shot me. Then he called George.

"Why don't you call the *Chronicle* while you're at it?" Marie shouted from the kitchen. I had to admire her verve, but I couldn't because I passed out again.

When I awoke, I was freshly bandaged on head and arm. Marie, seeing my eyes open, told me to sit up and when I did, she put a glass of water to my lips. "I suppose you should have an IV, but you don't seem to be in shock. Your temperature is okay. Your blood pressure is a little tricky, I admit. But you're tough. It's just a flesh wound. The bullet went through. Drink up."

Then Stella was there. I felt she was looking at me with new respect. "You and Marie? How long has this been going on?"

Why was everyone so interested in the length?

I decided to make it longer than her and young Derek. "Three months," I said.

"But ... have we even known the Steins that long? Didn't we meet the night of your birthday?"

I shrugged, which hurt like hell.

Probably Stella was jealous, not because of the affair, but because she herself had never got to shoot me.

Marie was smiling and Alvin glowered.

"Why did you shoot him?" Stella asked Marie.

"He deserved it," she said crisply.

Then George and Laurie arrived. "Ears, are you all right?" He leaned down and gave me a kiss. Bless him. Good old George. "We had no idea about you and Marie,' he said. "If I'd known, I would have warned you she's impetuous. She shoots first and asks questions later." He laughed. Marie smiled her enigmatic smile. Stella frowned and Alvin was making an art form of the glower.

"He must have been hiding in the house," Alvin said peevishly, "waiting for me to leave, but I was only walking Flintstone. He thought I'd left for the day. But, wait a minute ..."

The poor guy would never figure it out. Whereas I bet Marie already had. She was so smart. Also, there were shards of pink china sticking through my pockets. "Well," I said groggily, "Looks like everyone got here early for the cocktail party."

I decided this would definitely count as a Return, even if I didn't present them with the broken pieces. Tim's Rules of Return.

Four down, five to go.

XVII

FINISHED

I was buoyed from being shot, especially after twelve hours of sleep. I felt happier than I had in a long time. I felt like I *had* been having a love affair with Marie and that my life was full of drama and romance.

The pain, however, was not insignificant. I took three Advils after I shaved. When I came upstairs, Stella was there, and I was touched that she was. Maybe she would make my breakfast for me. Over breakfast I would tell her the truth about Marie and about the flamingoes. We would make a new start together. I would try to be more cheerful, more kind. I would say I was devastated over her love affair and beg her to come back to me, be wholly mine as before. Why not? Why not admit my true feelings?

The spurt of hot, glorious days had ended. Outside, a gauzy fog veiled the mountain and hung over the lagoon water where a scattering of buffle-head ducks dived up and down like a Disney sequence. Gulls winged past the window, making their cat cries.

Stella made no move to bestir herself in the kitchen. Awkwardly, using my left hand, I got the coffee machine underway, stood by it waiting. She sat in the living room rocking chair. I could see her over the counter, facing me, still in her bathrobe, her expression sour.

Dispensing with Good Morning, How Are You Feeling, she said, as if in mid-conversation, "When I was honest with you about Derek, don't you think that would have been the time to tell me about Marie?"

"No, because, you see ..."

"I suppose you are all full of yourself because you have a psychiatrist lover and mine is a salesman."

I smiled. "I guess I didn't realize it was a contest. But, listen, Stella ..."

"Well, she's forty-five years old if she's a day."

"Okay, so you win the lover youth contest, I win the brains."

"She's not going to be bearing you any children if that's what you had hoped."

Suddenly I didn't want to tell her how much I loved her. "Can you hear yourself when you say things like that?" I was really curious.

"Yes I can and I'm not proud of myself. The words just pop out. I think the reason is ..."

"Tourette's syndrome?"

"No. It's that I hate you."

I poured my coffee with shaking hands. "Why do you hate me?" Feeling I needed sustenance fast, I drank coffee, burning my tongue. But what was a little more pain in the already overburdened system?

She told me why. "I can't forgive you. For a long time I didn't remember any of the details about Jamie's death. I mean, the hospital part. I know you had forgotten, too. Then, recently I started remembering. Have you?"

I was silent.

"Listen. Here's how it was. You insisted on bringing him home. The doctor wanted to keep him there for observation. George agreed with him, but you had to have him home with you. George even said you could stay with Jamie all night at the hospital, but no, as usual, your possessiveness of Jamie was extreme. If he had stayed, he'd probably still be alive. He'd be with us now."

I was stunned. She looked like she believed what she was saying. She was looking right at me, dead serious. Her eyes were opaquely bright, like glass eyes, teddy bear eyes. Her voice trembled a little toward the end when she openly swore that Jamie might still be with us, were it not for me.

"I wasn't going to tell you. Why pile more misery onto you? But it was eating me up. I felt more and more resentful, and now, this thing with Marie. Well, I didn't sleep much last night and I decided to get it all off my breast. I thought, maybe Tim won't be so busy playing the bereaved father if he finds out the hand he played in our tragedy."

All I could think was, thank God I know it's not true. Thank God for Laurie telling me about the hospital scene. If I had believed Stella, I would have killed myself on the spot. As it was, I felt like killing myself rather than admit that my once-beloved Stella could be this cruel, crueler than death itself.

I remembered the night she had talked drunkenly about the devil's pact. Maybe that was when she had remembered the truth and then, finding it intolerable, had twisted it around. One part of me still wanted to embrace her, hold her to my heart, tell her it was all right, that Jamie was gone, but we had each other, and we would survive because it was nobody's fault, least of all ours. Death came and took people. He took our boy. Nothing could have prevented it. The Lord taketh.

But the other part of me was ascendant, the part that recoiled from her. I felt I never wanted her in my arms or anywhere near me. Once again, I was going to vomit. I made it to the kitchen sink. Burning my throat, it burst from my mouth. She watched me coldly. "I heard about your vomiting the night of my show, right outside on the sidewalk, showing your true feelings for my work and your unhappiness at my success."

I rinsed out my mouth. When I was able to talk, I said, "You can have the houseboat. You and Derek. I'm leaving. Give me a week to get organized. Stay with Derek in the meantime so I don't have to see you."

Something like panic came to her eyes.

"How can I live with a woman who hates me, who is trying to destroy me? I try to tell myself you don't mean to be cruel, but now I know that you do. Maybe it is a sickness in you that will pass. I hope so, for your sake. But I'll be long gone. I'm going to leave the country and never come back."

I didn't know I was going to say that, do that, but now it seemed the right thing. I felt some of the beneficence that I'd felt upon awakening return to my battered self. I would spend my life wandering from place to place with Jamie in my heart. I headed for the door as if anxious to get going with the wandering at once. She stood up and stretched out her hands. "Wait. Stop. I'm sorry. I went too far. It's true. I just can't seem to help myself these days. I say these awful things without thinking, wanting to hurt you. But I don't want to live with Derek. And I don't want to be alone. Don't leave me, Tim. It's just that I was hurt about Marie. And jealous. I love you. Only you."

"I thought I could never leave you. You were all I had left, but it was enough, was everything to me. But you are not the woman you were, or that I believed you were."

"Because I am not Marie?"

"Marie and I are not lovers. Everyone just jumped to that conclusion. I was only returning the two flamingoes I had stolen from her kitchen, but that's beside the point now."

"Were they real flamingoes?" she asked, trying to be funny, and it was funny, or would have been, but for all that had gone before. Still, I couldn't help but feel touched that she would try to make this joke that I had made twice on her, and make a truce thereby. But I also felt angry that she would try to lighten this incredibly grave moment of my ending it forever, by being so flip, being so much the way I always was. So I continued to walk out the door, out of her life.

"You'll forgive me, Tim. You always do," she called out before the door shut behind me. And I heard her say, in muffled words behind the door, "You have to," which could have meant she would be lost without me, but more likely meant she thought I would be lost without her. Which would have been true a half hour ago, but no longer was. The way it was now, I was lost with her.

There was a small Thai restaurant across the street from the dock parking lot. I headed for there. They had the best French toast in the world, made with sourdough bread with crushed pecans on top.

My arm was sore and my head hurt and my stomach was still in knots from the scene with Stella, but my good spirits were returning. Everything was over now. Stella and I were finished. Nothing more to lose. Starting from scratch now. Once the flamingoes were returned, I would take off for parts unknown. Over the years to come I would send postcards to Joy so she wouldn't forget me and Jamie. Maybe she'd keep them in a special box. Maybe they would be important to her. She wouldn't be able to bring Uncle Tim to mind, or Jamie, but she'd have probably hundreds of postcards of the world's most marvelous sights, hopefully with something meaningful written on the back of them. For sure George would love them and go often to the special box to finger them lovingly. Maybe I should send George his own postcards.

During breakfast, having scanned the paper and found no more articles on Angley, the reporter presumably having leeched all the humor out of it for the time being, I made my plan for the day. I would go to the Zeus offices, ostensibly to get the box of things that had been cleaned out of my office, return the stolen flamingo mug, then hie myself to the Catholic church's rummage shop to return the spoon-holder. I would have lunch, grab a nap at Jamie's house, then decide how to return Ugly to Jack's Alleged Antiques ie: Jackass Jack's Jaded Junk, although the ride over the mountain would be hell on my sore arm. And head. And ass from when the skateboarder felled me, never mind the glass-ground groin. Face it! The returns were not going well so far. I thought they would be so easy. But today's mission seemed simple and straightforward, especially if I didn't go to Stinson. I was leery of Jack, very leery. Never mind. I would just take it one flamingo at a time.

Once in the car, I called George as I had promised to do, to tell him how I was feeling. He was in the operating room again so I left a message with his service. Then I figured I had better call Marie.

"I'm very sorry," I told her when we were connected. "I hope you and Alvin are okay."

"He calmed down at last. After all, there was the broken window as proof of an intruder. I told him you were probably returning the flamingo set, a story George corroborated although he didn't realize you'd taken some of ours. Do be careful with the other returns."

"I will."

"Are you all right?"

"I feel better emotionally than I have in a long time. Sort of galvanized."

"It's the excitement. You may come down hard in a day or two, or sooner. Pay attention. How is Stella?"

"Well ..."

"Go ahead."

"It's over."

"Do you want me to talk to her?"

"No. It isn't about us. It's about Jamie."

"I'm sorry, Tim." She allowed us one of her blessed silences. Then, "You'd be surprised how many couples break up over the loss of a child, something like eighty-five percent. There has to be a powerful lot of love and trust to survive."

"I thought there was."

"It has to be on both sides."

"Right."

"Look, when you return the other flamingoes, instead of trying to sneak it back where it was when you took it, just go up to the person and return it. You don't have to explain, apologize, or defend yourself. Don't you think that's the best way?"

It wasn't surprising that she didn't understand The Importance of the Correct Return.

"It was just a thought. Anyhow, get some rest today. Watch that you don't run a fever. Drink water."

"Yes, Ma'am."

"Have George check the wound. I was rather slapdash with the sutures."

"Thanks, Marie. You're wonderful."

"I know."

Next I dialed Betsy. "I have a present for you. An egg."

"*Faberge,* I hope."

"Not quite, although it is an art egg. Think *Faberge* without the jewels, or the price." I waited for her to say something about Angley. Maybe

146

she didn't read the paper. Some people didn't. But she had Jack for her newsmonger. She was always talking to Jack.

"Jack said ..."

"Something about Angley, no doubt."

"Yes, a detective Angley hired came and asked him if he had a Porsche. He was checking out all the bidders."

"Why did Jack bid on them?" I was still curious about that.

"He wanted them."

"Does Jack know that I have a Porsche?"

"He didn't."

'But you told him, right?" She told Jack everything, just as I told George everything and George told Laurie, Marie, and the man on the street everything.

"Tim," Betsy asked, "Are you the flamingo thief?"

It amazed me that she had to ask.

"No longer. I'm returning them. I'm returning Jack's today, tomorrow at the latest. I'll be returning Angley's, too. It will be so long to all of us feeling anguish for old Angley in Angwin."

"How many are there?"

"Nine. Not counting your gift."

"Angley has set a trap, Tim, according to the Times. He'll probably catch you. Why don't you just call him the hell up and tell him you have it."

This was an even more simplistic method than Marie's suggestion that I go up to the person and calmly give it to them. This way it is hardly returned at all. I telephone them and they come and collect it. How impure can you get? These women!

147

"You could go to prison for this. And it's so stupid. I know it's because you're grieving. It takes people weird ways. Look, maybe I could help you. I can at least return Jack's for you."

The Most Impure Return of all!

"No, thanks. It's up to me. You see, it turns out it is actually harder to return them than to steal them. Yesterday, during the commission of the un-crime, I got shot."

Horrified and fascinated, she exclaimed aloud, making sounds much like her coitus call. I gave her the rudiments of the story, once again feeling buoyant, important, and overexcited. She, like the others, right away believed I was Marie's lover. "So this is why you bought me the egg — to appease me. Well, it's not going to work. I know we didn't have any kind of understanding. I know I wasn't much more than a one-night stand – or two-afternoon stand. And I knew you were married and that you loved your wife. But to have a mistress, too, Tim, is beyond the pale."

"Why do people equate being shot with being in love?"

"Because when it is real people, not gangsters, it's always about love, or lack of love."

"I don't have a mistress and I don't even have a wife anymore."

"I don't blame them. We're finished, too, Tim, if we ever even began. I don't like cheaters and I don't like thieves. I thought you were so nice."

"You are too good for me, anyhow, Betsy. By the way, you're too good for Jack, too."

"Jack and I will never be finished."

"He's very lucky."

"Thank you. I kind of still would like to have the art egg, for a memento."

"First I have to return all the flamingoes. Then I'll come and say goodbye. I'm going away to the ends of the earth."

XVIII

FRANK'S FLAMINGOES

I drove to Zeus Juice. Driving was difficult but my shift arm was not the damaged one, and when I shifted, I could sort of hold the steering wheel with the bad arm or with my knees.

There was no longer a parking space with my name on it. Once inside, I was amazed and touched to be greeted so warmly by the staff, and to hear expressions of sadness at my no longer adorning the place. I got my box of stuff that had been cleared from my office, put the flamingo mug inside, and made small talk with the new president who was overly hearty and who was wearing new, pressed, non-Levi jeans, blindingly blue, so stiff he could hardly bend his knees.

I went to the desk whence I had spotted and taken the flamingo mug. The woman sitting there looked familiar, but not from seeing her around the company. She was a small, tidy, woman, Asian, with a stylish haircut and vibrant face. My mind blanked the way it does when you see someone out of context then I realized it was Lisa Barnes, Jimmy's mom.

"Hello, Tim. I can see you're surprised to see me here. I'm new."

"Hi, Lisa. How are you? I had a great time kayaking with Jimmy and Paul."

"They enjoyed it, too. Thank you."

"How long have you been working here?"

"Just a few weeks."

"Then this isn't your mug."

Lisa paled. "Oh, dear. It's the flamingo mug."

"What's the matter with it?"

"It belonged to the woman who was here before me. She lost her job because of it. It went missing and she started accusing everyone, even the boss, especially the boss, because he was working late that Friday. As a result, he fired her."

"I borrowed it one Saturday when I was here." I gestured at the box of knick-knacks, which I had set on her desk. "It got in with my things."

This was a nasty situation in itself but what made it uncomfortable for me was that I'd taken Lisa's toothpick-holder flamingo and it was extremely possible that Lisa knew that and was thinking about it even as we discussed this other disappeared flamingo from my ex-office.

I looked deep into her eyes to see what knowledge lurked there and she blushed, but maybe just because of my overly searching gaze, not because she knew I was a flamingo thief. They were nice eyes and she was a nice woman. Her own flamingo was slated for a Return tomorrow, which would be the fourth day since the final, highly publicized theft, the one that had so anguished Angley. Hers was the only one that had not been stolen by stealth. I had only to replace it on her kitchen table in the same spirit in which I had picked it up and pocketed it – as if it were mine to begin with.

Meanwhile, this poor, fired woman had to be found and things made right. I remembered her now. She was an older woman and I imagined a howible scenario whereby she had lost her apartment after losing her job and was now on the streets, a homeless person, all because of me.

"Hilda told me she was glad to be fired and that anyhow the company wouldn't be the same with you gone. She said it was going to hell. They gave her two months' wages."

"I'll give her a year's wages since it was my fault."

"Well, it wasn't your fault that she accused the new CEO."

"That's worth a year's wages right there." We laughed together. And she said she would get me Hilda's address. She left the desk and soon returned with it. We said goodbye and again she thanked me for the day with the boys.

I began to think I should make an arrangement to see her so I wouldn't have to break into her house or, using the kids, go through the door behind her back. "Would you like to have dinner together tomorrow? I owe you for your kindness the other night when I came and cried."

"Aren't you married, Tim?"

"I didn't mean it as a date exactly."

"I can't tomorrow anyhow, thanks."

It had to be tomorrow if I was going to get Angley's back tomorrow, too. Hers was the one before Angley's. I couldn't wait for the fifth day. The detective would have nabbed me by then. "It has to be tomorrow," I said, not desperately but a bit sternly, as a king might speak before he'd been dethroned.

"Oh."

"How about lunch?" No. No. She'd be here at work. That was no good. Could I do it today? The Return of the spoon holder would be easy and next was Ugly, which would be hard but not impossible. Yes, today – tonight, rather, was barely possible. I pursued the idea.

"Or how about tonight? That would work." (I should not have said that would work.) "I could come by and bring dessert for you and the boys. Tonight at eight?" Again she said no.

She said, "I'm sorry."

"This would be sexual harassment if I were still the boss here, but thank God I'm not. So," I smiled hopefully, with the charm I was famous for, but was fast losing, because of being a felon, and having a sore arm from being shot, "how about tonight at nine?"

She began to laugh. "Oh, all right, since you are so insistent, and since it *has* to be today or tomorrow. See you at nine, then. Anything to get rid of you so I can get some work done around here." She laughed again. It was nice to be with someone who laughed. Even Betsy, who was so cheerful, didn't laugh out loud. And to hear my own laugh issuing from my mouth instead of burning vomit was a treat. It reminded me of my old self, my old, old self.

I wrote a check for thirty thousand dollars and put it in the flamingo mug for Hilda. It occurred to me I should also pay Arnold for the broken Dagwood, not a year's wages, but something.

When I arrived at Hilda's condominium in Novato, one town north from San Rafael, I found her at home. She was a middle-aged, heavy woman in good faded Levi jeans, what I call four-star jeans. After four stars, jeans go directly downhill from faded to threadbare and become zero stars, which are what new jeans are, and store-bought-faded, which are easily detectible as pseudo-faded, are also zero stars. There are no one-star or two-star jeans. Three stars are excellent. Most of mine are three-star jeans carefully husbanded. My two four-stars are for supremely special occasions because their days are so sadly numbered. Some jeans wearers think that threadbare and holey is even more fashionable than perfectly soft and faded but they are wrong. Threadbare is zero-starred. I won't even discuss store-bought holey and threadbare.

I gave Hilda the mug and check and the explanation. She was delighted and, in return, gave me a cup of coffee, plus a half-hour of good conversation. We were square.

Onwards. Next stop was the Mt. Carmel Salvage Shop in Mill Valley to return the Sixth Flamingo. First I went to a bakery on the same block and got a turkey sandwich to- go and a cake for Lisa and her boys. They boxed it up and I put it in the trunk. I put the sandwich in the glove compartment for later.

At the salvage shop, I lay the flamingo on a shelf that displayed other china items, no one the wiser. This constituted the Easiest Return, simple and smooth, without a hitch. Then, glancing down the stairway, who should I see but old Muttonchops himself, rummaging through the salvage, finding items he could take home, put his rust-and-dust machine on, and sell for ten times what he would pay for them here.

I nipped out the door before he spotted me. It was a shame I didn't know what his car looked like. Ugly was slated for the next return. I could glue it on the hood and it would save me the drive to Stinson. Ugly, with his extreme coloration, outstretched wings, high-held head, would look great as a hood ornament.

My demolished body was pulling the big fade. I determined to head for Jamie's house where I could take more pills, eat, and sleep. It was one o'clock.

I awoke on the glider almost three hours later. It was four o'clock. I felt as if I had been hit by a sledgehammer. I went to the kitchen to take more Advil. My arm and head were killing me, and those pains seemed to reinvent the pain of my knee from the beach chase and of my butt from being dashed to the ICB floor by the skateboarder. I was a wreck. I felt about a hundred years old.

Passing through the living room, I said groggily, "Something is wrong here." Washing down the pills, I said, more alertly, "Something is seriously wrong about the house. What is it?"

My eyes roved around. Oh, that was it. There were no flamingoes. The house looked tragically bare. No happy spots of pink. No pretty statuettes to charm the roving eye.

I ambled back into the living room: Oak floors, brick fireplace, beautiful windows, French doors. I slapped my hand to my forehead. No flamingoes was right. Not even Final. Here was where Final had stood like the Majority Leader of the Senate, and Final was gone. Disappeared. Good grief!

I dashed from room to room even though I knew I'd left it in the living room. Had it been here when I came for my nap? I couldn't remember. I'd been so tired. I didn't even go into the house proper, just headed for the porch glider to wolf my sandwich then lay down to sleep. I was out like a light. But it could have been taken yesterday or the day before.

Impossible. No one knew about this house. Except George. Yes, yes, what a relief. It had to be George. Probably he decided to help me by returning it to Angwin himself, knowing I'd insist on keeping to The Order of Return, and seeing how long it was taking me, and figuring that being shot would delay me even further. He'd been so hipped on getting it back to Angley, post haste. Yes, yes, that was it. George. Being the unfailingly protective older brother, seeing precious time hastening by, the detective hot on my heels, he had stepped in once again to save my neck.

I felt relieved but then was flooded by new anxiety. What about the trap? George would easily fall into Angley's trap. He was so unwitting. I envisioned a hole in the ground, covered with a sheer fabric of fake earth so that, as the quarry, George, jauntily stepped forward, he would fall in and be impaled by a stake. Or, it could be an actual animal trap with steel teeth that grab your ankle? Or, worse, one of those where you trip a wire and are hoisted aloft by a noose falling around your neck.

I ran to my car for the cell phone.

George was home. "I'll be right over," I said.

"Uncle Tim, have you come to play?"

Joy launched herself into my arms and I grabbed her with my good arm and sat her on my hip, her legs around my waist. "No. I've got to talk to your Daddy, honey. Serious business."

"And then we'll play?"

"We'll see."

"Is it Blimey Night?"

"Was it? I'd lost track. Had I watered the blimeys this morning? No. The fight with Stella. But it was foggy. They liked that better than water. Had Stella left by now? Would Joy ever see her room?

I closeted myself with George in his library/office and told him about the missing flamingo and my belief (hope) that he'd taken it from Jamie's house and returned it to Angley. He hadn't.

"Now I feel like a crummy brother that I didn't do that."

"I'm glad you didn't. I was so afraid you would be hurt in his trap."

"I've let you down, Ears, when you needed me most. But all the shooting excitement put it out of my mind — the shooting and my intense jealousy over your being Marie's lover which I now understand not to be the case."

"Are you her lover?"

"No, but I always wanted to be. I want to be everyone's lover, but especially Marie's. But, forget that. Who took your flamingo?"

I remembered seeing Jack at the salvage shop and told George about him, how I'd stolen a flamingo from his shop, later had a fleeting love affair with a woman who turned out to be Jack's wife, and how both of them knew I was the flamingo thief, Porsche driver, auction goer, and all-round idiot.

"Goddamn it, Ears, this secret life of yours! I thought I had problems. It must be genetic."

"Jack bid. He wanted the flamingoes. I saw him earlier today. By now he knows I have one of them and he could have followed me home to get it from me. I was so exhausted, he could have stomped into the house blowing a trumpet and I wouldn't have heard him.

"That house has so many doors and half the time one or two are unlocked, not to mention the windows," George said.

"George, I have to go to the Stinson shop anyhow to return the one I stole from him. Do you want to come?"

"Can I drive?"

"You have to drive."

"Let me check your wound. Can Joy and Flintstone come too? We can walk on the beach after."

"Of course!"

George re-dressed the bullet wound, making little clicking sounds over the sutures. He also scrutinized my head wound. I drank water. Then we gathered up dog and child and got in the car, Flintstone at my feet, Joy on my lap, belted in with me. I reminded Joy how Flintstone disliked driving with the top down. "You have to comfort him."

Joy said severely, "He has to get used to it, Uncle Tim."

That brought tears to my eyes because it assumed a future of us all driving together. But I was going away. Jamie and I were going away to the ends of the earth. Sending postcards.

Then I had my first-ever vision of Jamie. I could see him through the windshield, sitting on the hood of this car he didn't know I had. George hadn't started the engine yet, was still belting in.

Jamie said, "*I don't want to leave home, Dad.*"

"Jamie!" I cried joyfully, but he was already fading. "Jamie!"

I turned to George excitedly. "I just saw Jamie."

"Oh, Tim. I should have taken your temperature."

"He was sitting on the hood of the car." When I saw tears come to my brother's eyes, I assured him, "It was a good sighting. He looked terrific. His wonderful smile. I heard his voice, too."

"Me saw him too, Daddy," Joy said, and I hugged her close for her love and her belief.

George started the car and before we had gone a block, I dropped off to sleep. When I awoke, we were on the mountain's down-slope to the beach. Now Joy was sleeping. Flintstone, too.

George and I talked. He told me he was celibate now and going three times a week to Green Gulch monastery to study Zen Buddhism. "For the first time in my life, I'm beginning to begin not to feel restless."

"I'm happy for you."

Then I told George about Stella and how it had come to pass that we were through. "Thank God that Laurie told me about the hospital scene, that it was Stella, not me, who insisted on taking Jamie home."

"I told her never to tell you."

"But, don't you see, if she hadn't, I would have believed Stella, that it was my fault."

"What was? Jamie dying? Is it Stella's fault?"

"No. I don't blame Stella. Not at all. But I do blame her for lying to me about it. I blame her for saying it was because of me Jamie didn't stay in the hospital where he would, might, have been safe."

"But, Tim," George said gently. "She might have wanted him home for your sake and knew you'd be unable to ask for it. Maybe she did it for you. And now in her mind, she sees it as you who did it. Stella was, is, always able to play the bad guy for you, knowing that you can't. That's the kind of couple you are. A married couple consists of three people: you, the wife, and the couple itself, which acts in concert as one person."

"But didn't I try to stop her from taking Jamie home from the hospital?"

"Not really."

Betsy was presiding over Jack's shop when I entered with George, Joy and Flintstone. Flintstone, having tackled the difficult stairs, stood there with his tongue lolling. I introduced everyone. Betsy asked Joy how she liked her bedroom furniture and Joy was bewildered as was George. Flushing, I explained to George that I had made a little bedroom for Joy on the houseboat. George looked sad and said "That was so nice of you, wasn't it Joy?"

"Can I spend tonight there, Uncle Tim?"

"Maybe not tonight, but soon. Next Blimey Night." When would that be, if Stella kept the houseboat? When, if I went away? What about the blimeys and Captain Rick? They needed me and I them. I've always loved and needed fruit. Who would take care of them? Not Stella and Derek. But Jamie, from the hood of the car, said he didn't want us to go away. I shook my head, feeling so confused. Maybe I did have a fever.

"Is tonight Blimey Night?" Joy asked her father, hopefully.

"Every night is Blimey Night," he answered, Zen-like.

Betsy looked from one to the other of us. She said, "Blimey?"

Flintstone started to sneeze. "It's the dust," I said. "Why don't I meet you guys on the beach in fifteen minutes?"

They left the shop and I wandered to the rear to put Ugly approximately where it was when I snatched it. It shone there among the dreary, dust-laden objects. "'Bye, Ugly," I said quietly.

Back up at the front of the store, I said to Betsy, "I think Jack took Angley's flamingo from my house. I've got to get it back so I can return it."

She took a phone from her dress pocket. It was littler than mine. Everyone tries to get smaller phones than the next guy has. Soon they'll be the size of peanuts. "I'll call and ask him."

"How many times have you talked to him today?"

"Three or four."

"Did he say anything to you about going to my house?"

"No. But nowadays he tries not to tell me things I disapprove of, that would upset me."

"Do you try not to upset him? I mean, does he know about us?"

"He certainly saw you kiss me goodbye at the auction. But that is all he knows. Which is a lot, actually. But it probably wouldn't make him any madder than stealing his flamingo. He was burned."

"I didn't hold it aloft, by the way."

"What?"

"Nothing."

"Did you bring my egg?"

"I didn't know you'd be here." Where was Arnold's egg? I had no idea. I hardly knew where I was. Arnold's anguished egg.

She dialed, spoke a few hushed words to her husband then handed me the phone.

"Jack, this is Tim Forester. I'm calling from your shop."

"Where you are probably pillaging more of my wares. Hold on while I call the police on the other line."

"Very funny. Now, listen. I saw you at the Mt. Carmel Salvage shop today. Did you see me? Did you follow me home and take Angley's flamingo while I was sleeping?"

"Everyone's on my ass about that fucking flamingo."

"Because you wanted it."

"I wanted the pair. That's why Angley said they're inseparable. The pair's worth more than the misprint in the paper. Add another zero. "

"One hundred and twenty thousand!"

"Yeah. Only an idiot like you wouldn't know that and would just steal the one, which is worthless without the other. You see, these flamingoes were designed by Frank Lloyd Wright for a small hotel he did in the Bahamas which is no longer extant. I knew I couldn't outbid Angley, but you could have. I thought you were waiting to come in at the end of the bidding with a sizeable sum. Then I would have worked something out with you. But no, you're just a neurotic, rich guy who takes flamingoes for the fun of it."

"I don't think Angley knows their value either. His house is full of animal statuettes of all kinds. I think he said they were inseparable because he anthropormorphizes them, thinks they're human."

"Thanks for defining the word for me. Man, you are such a jerk."

"So, you're saying you didn't take the flamingo from me."

"I don't know where your houseboat is and Betsy wouldn't tell me."

"Well, I just put back your flamingo which, by the way, I never held aloft when I was running with it."

"You can bet your ass you did."

"I can bet my ass, but you couldn't catch my ass." I clicked off the phone, mourning the lost days when you could slam down the receiver. It wasn't even a click, more a psst.

XIX

FAMILIES

It was now seven o'clock and I had to be at Lisa Barnes' house at nine. This was turning into a fabulous four flamingo day and, so far, no mishaps, except for the one flamingo costing me thirty thousand dollars. Also, there was the rather enormous problem of the missing flamingo, the most important one to return if I was not to go to prison instead of to the ends of the earth.

I found George, Joy, and Flintstone on the beach where a few surfers plied the last waves of the day, but no swimmers. There were almost never swimmers in these freezing waters. George was throwing sticks into the water, shouting, "Go get it, Flintstone. Good dog. Atta boy." Flintstone remained stolid about not chasing them. Instead, he sat and looked adoringly at George, happy that throwing sticks gave him pleasure. Joy was running back and forth like a tiny maniac, reveling in her power to make flocks of seagulls explode into the air, imitating their cries. Meanwhile, a sunset was announced in the form of a pale, pink tinge infusing the bleached sky. From now on, when I needed to see pink, I had only to look at the sunset. Hassle-free pink.

I filled George in on the latest. "So Jack didn't take it and no one but you knows I still have the Mill Valley house. It seems unlikely that a passing burglar happened on it. I'm bewildered."

"When I'm bewildered, I eat. Let's check out Parkside, see if it's open."

At the side of the park that was between the village and the beach was a great burger stand and, thanks to summer hours, it was still open although we were bumping up against September. We all, including Flintstone, had the classic cheeseburger and fries with ice-cream softees for dessert, vanilla/chocolate combos. We sat at a picnic table. I stopped feeling bewildered and feverish and just felt happy to be with George and Joy, with Flintstone's head on my foot, happy to hear the rolling waves connect with the shore and see the color spread through the sky.

Then George, having eaten, came up with a brilliant explanation of the missing Final. "I've got it figured, Ears. Listen. If Angley's detective got your name from, say, Jack, he could look in the county computers, find out what property you own, and check out both houses for the flamingo. He shouldn't have entered the house but he probably saw it was empty, open, and thought what the hell, especially since he could see the bird through the window."

"Right. Then he figured he'd just take it and return it to Angley."

"In which case he couldn't have you charged because it's no longer in your possession."

"Sounds good. I like it. But how do we find out if Angley's got it back?"

"You call and tell him you're a reporter from the *New York Times* following up the story."

"You're a genius. I'll call him in the morning. It would be too late for the *Times* to call tonight."

George drove back over the mountain in twenty minutes, a Boxster record. I washed up at his house, kissed Joy and Flintstone goodbye, shot down some more Advil, and was on my way to Lisa's with ten minutes to spare.

The canyon was full of cars. I had to park several blocks away — although the canyon had no blocks since it had no sidewalks. It was now night, but the starlight and moon glow did not penetrate the canyon's canopy of redwood branches by very much, nor were there any streetlights to speak of. Walking along, I was back to feeling weak and dazed despite my two naps and countless pain pills. Definitely this day was going on too long. A four flamingo day was a big one for a wounded Returner. However, at Lisa's, all I'd have to do was sit at her kitchen table, eat cake, then be on my way.

I turned up the drive, traversed the walk, rang the doorbell, and a strange man opened the door fast upon my ring. He waited and I waited, too. I waited for him to unblock the door and let me by. Was this the ex-husband? He looked fairly brutal for a Seventh Day Adventist teacher.

Gesturing at the cake box, which dangled from my hand by the string at the top, he asked, "Is this a delivery?"

"No, it's dessert for Lisa and the boys. She's expecting me."

"Lisa and the boys?"

"Look, I'm not up to this back and forth. Is she home or not? If she is, let me in, okay?"

He looked amused, not to the point of smiling but to where he seemed to relax his muscles. "I think you've got the wrong place, pal."

It hit me that this was the orgy house and perversely, or un-perversely, my dick got hard at the thought. I found myself trying to peer around the doorkeeper's formidable shoulders, but the minutes were ticking by and I had to go to Lisa's, no question.

"I forgot the password," I told him, trying for an insouciant tone and pose although it was tricky to achieve with the dangling cake box at the end of one arm and the other, wounded arm, dangling for no apparent reason.

"Password?"

Maybe it wasn't the orgy house.

In any case, my dick wilted as Brutenik turned me around and gave me a shove. The door closed behind me smartly.

I floundered around for another five minutes then found her house which, helpfully, said Barnes on the mailbox. A flagstone path. Hydrangeas. Right.

Jimmy met me at the door and whispered hectically, "Don't tell my Mom anything," and then Lisa was there, greeting me, accepting the cake, ushering me into the kitchen.

She wore khaki shorts and a pink tee shirt and looked pretty, but disturbed. The earlier fun and laughter as witnessed at Zeus Juice offices, had deserted her big-time. "Jimmy's in hot water," she said.

"Oh?" I darted a glance at him and he just shook his head warningly as if my even saying 'oh' was too much.

She served coffee and cut up the cake. I tried to remember when Stella had last served me coffee and cake and couldn't. But when had I last bought her a cake? Paul appeared, said hello, eyed the cake, and she told him to finish his homework first. She was tough. Then she spoke her mind, pinning me to my chair with a merciless eye.

"Have you read in the paper about this flamingo business?"

"No," I responded without having to look to Jimmy for the prompt.

She gave me a précis of all the newspaper articles then, sitting down, continued by saying, "Jimmy was in Angwin that weekend, which was last weekend. Also, he drove Mr. Angley to the auction where he bought the flamingoes and then drove him home again. Mr. Angley did not pay him what he promised for the day's work. Jimmy complained to his father, suggesting he invite the man over for a drink and wheedle the rest of the money out of him. While his father kindly carried out this commission, one of the flamingoes was stolen from Mr. Angley's house.

"Why it did not occur to Mr. Angley or to Jimmy's father that Jimmy had taken it as a prank, I can not imagine. It would have taken me about two seconds to figure it out, but I wasn't told about it. Mr. Angley got it in his mind that the thief was a man who had bid on the flamingoes, and he connected this man with the Porsche driver who had followed him home, so he hired a detective to find the guy. The detective found all the bidders but none of them had the tell-tale Porsche – some new model with a funny name."

She paused for a rapid sip of coffee, still looking at me.

"After a few days, the obvious finally occurred to him, that it was Jimmy. Angley told Jimmy's father. Jimmy's father called to shout at me about it because, of course, any child's misbehavior is essentially the mother's fault, according to the father. Mr. Angley has given Jimmy until midnight tonight to bring it back, but Jimmy says he didn't take it and doesn't have it."

"Don't you believe him?"

"Frankly, no."

"But ..."

"Jimmy has something of a history with Mr. Angley. He should never have accepted the job in the first place, but he needed the money."

Because of George's beautiful County Computers Theory, I was able to say stoutly, "I believe Jimmy. In fact, thinking it all over, I would not be surprised if Angley has gotten it back already but is too embarrassed to say so, because of all the fuss he created around it."

"Really?" It was heartbreaking how hopeful Lisa looked. We all so want our kids to be as innocent as the lilies in the field.

I looked past her at Jimmy, who made wild eyes, and shook his head in the negative while mouthing 'no'.

167

Jimmy seemed to be signaling that no, Angley did not have the flamingo back. No, I was all wet with my theory, George's theory that I had embraced with relief — the perfectly pure explanation, in the forwarding of which I had already mentally practiced being the *New York Times'* reporter for my morning call to Angley. No.

But Jimmy didn't know what I knew which was that the flamingo was no longer in my possession. When he knew that, he would begin to love George's theory.

"Lisa, do you mind if I speak to Jimmy privately?"

She frowned, but reluctantly said yes. Jimmy and I left the room. 'Outside," he whispered. "Otherwise, she'll hear."

Outside, I told him the flamingo was gone and zestfully began outlining my morning move, but he interrupted me, rapidly pouring out his story, so fast I could hardly follow, already staggered by his first words: *I have the flamingo.*

"I have the flamingo. Paul knew where Jamie's house was and didn't know you had moved. The flamingo was inside. I knew the blame was going to come down on me and since you had told me you were going to get it back, but not right away because of being compulsive, I decided to take the return into my own hands. I grabbed it this morning and I've been waiting for mom to get home with the car, but she was late and then she was furious from talking to Dad and put me On Bounds, meaning I can't leave the house. You'd think, if she's so damn sure I have it, she'd give me a chance to get it back under the deadline."

"But you lied and told her you didn't have it."

"Well … right, but…"

"Why don't I go and tell her the whole, real story."

"No, Tim. We still can get it back in time without anyone knowing the real story, and I promise you that's the best way to go."

"Where is it?"

"In the garage. Let's load it in the car and take off."

"That will look pretty strange, won't it, you and I taking off without a word to your mother?"

"What do you think we should do?"

If he only knew how I couldn't think straight, and how the idea of driving pell mell to Angwin and back fatigued me beyond belief, never mind trying to evade The Trap once we got there: the hidden hole in the ground, the spikes, the steel trap with teeth, or the trip-wire noose.

"Okay, Jimmy. I will tell your mother that I believe the hunchback is lying and that we are going there to confront him. You be loading the flamingo into the car and be waiting at the end of the drive with the car running."

"Cool! You're the best, Tim!"

"I'm the worst. This is all completely my fault."

"But don't say hunchback, or she'll know that you know him."

I returned to the kitchen, pulling myself together as best I could. She was standing, waiting, arms-akimbo, looking angry, as if I'd just arrived home drunk for the third night in a row. It's hard to be a single mother of boys.

"Jimmy and I are going to Angwin together to confront Mr. Angley with his outrageous lie. Could I have permission for Jimmy to leave the house?"

"No."

"No?" I spread my arms beseechingly. "Lisa, please?"

"The fact is, I don't really know you very well, Tim, and I don't fancy you taking my son off in the middle of the night on some escapade that doesn't make sense to me. Also, there seems to be something highly suspicious going on because there's a flamingo connection with you. Earlier today, that mug …"

"I didn't even know that mug had a flamingo on it until …"

She ignored me. "And the night you first came here, under very strange circumstances, I believe you took a little flamingo toothpick holder I had."

"This flamingo toothpick holder?" I withdrew it from my pocket and passed it to her, because I did have to make The Return before I left, and before I returned Angley's, because of The Order of Return. "Pure chance. I picked it up without thinking, having no idea it was embossed with a flamingo. It was a nervous gesture. I was thrown by your beauty."

She took the little fellow in her hands and was at a loss for words, which I think was unusual for her.

"Lisa, I promise you Jimmy is innocent and I am going to prove it." I turned and, well, I ran like hell from the room, from the house, down the walk, the drive, and leapt into the waiting car. Jimmy gunned it out of there.

That Return had gone pretty well, all in all, sort of, hard to say, actually. I'd have to review it in my mind tomorrow, if there was a tomorrow, if I still had a mind.

170

XX

FINAL FLAMINGO RETURN

Lisa's car was one of the hated Sport Utility Vehicles which have infested the county in recent years: giant gas-guzzling cars driven by persons with no passengers who feel that because of the greater size of their carapace, they don't need to signal or follow any other of the rules of the road, who think: why use one parking space when I can easily fit in two?

However, it was incredibly comfortable. "Jimmy, I'm just going to have a quick nap."

When I awoke, we were about thirty minutes from Angwin. I waited for my head to clear, then said "Jimmy, I have some explaining to do."

"First let me talk, Tim. I love to talk when I'm driving in the dark and don't have to look at the person I'm talking to. It's the only time I can talk, really. I mean, say anything important. But also I feel comfortable talking to you, particularly, even though you're the man I was scared to death of for a whole year.

"At the memorial service for Jamie, I was afraid to look at you. I felt so guilty, like a murderer. But I made myself look and it was the scariest face I ever saw. Even though you weren't looking at me, I thought to myself, he's going to kill me. When I told Mom and Dad how scared I was, they said they didn't think you would harm me but you might sue us for wrongful death and then we'd be ruined."

I looked over at his fine, young face in the semi-glow cast by the lights of the intersection we had stopped at. "They never should have told you such a thing."

"I wish they hadn't. It made me feel more guilt. First I ruin your family then I ruin mine. Also, after the accident, everything went to hell with our family. Dad left. Mom kept saying it had nothing to do with me. He fell in love with another woman. But I felt like it did have to do with me. Then we didn't have so much money because of the two households. Mom was good at getting jobs but she couldn't hold them. And she had to learn computers. She was never home.

"I got in with a ring of bicycle thieves. I was a good thief. I made money and I liked the excitement. But, eventually I got caught. First offense, so I got off with doing community work and paying a fine. But it killed Mom. Dad, too, probably, but I didn't care about him.

"So you can see why everyone's so steamed up about Angley's stupid flamingo and me being back to stealing again."

"Jimmy, I had every intention of stealing that flamingo before you even showed up at Ana's Cantina."

"Why?" He glanced over at me even though it was against his rules of driving and talking.

"I don't know. I've been stealing flamingoes all over the place, all summer long. It was fun. It made me feel better. It took my mind off Jamie. This last week I've been returning them all and it hasn't been easy. Last night I got shot."

Jimmy loved my getting-shot story and he told me some of his close calls with the bicycle thieving. Then we got serious again.

"Guilt is a terrible thing. I've felt grief about Jamie, but not guilt. My wife took on the guilt, maybe for both of us. I thought she was handling it all much better than me, but she wasn't. Recently, she's achieved success as an artist."

Jamie was right. It was great to talk while speeding through the dark, country night. The words came easily.

"That was her show you were telling us about the night you first appeared."

"Yes, but her success redoubled her guilt, because her art is about Jamie's death, which it has every right to be, but she feels she got what she wanted all her life, only over his dead body."

Saying this aloud seemed to put it straight. It made me understand Stella. "Jimmy, it's helping me to talk to you about it all."

"That's good."

"I think when I started stealing flamingoes, I pulled away from Stella. The flamingoes became the most important thing. I was possessed. She started having an affair and I was fooling around, too. It was a mess."

While we turned off the Silverado Trail and started the climb to Angwin, I continued thinking it over to myself, how I've hardly been home because of my flamingo hunting and stealing. But, even before that it was a mess. Not sleeping with her so I could talk to James. I could have talked to him silently. Why did it have to be aloud? Even when we made love, I would leave her afterward. Even when she asked me please to stay, I left. It was bad action.

The truth hit me in the face. *Talking to Stella was more important than talking to James!*

Jimmy said, "You think you're the only one who is messed up, but then you find out practically everyone has problems of some kind. A lot of my friends' parents are divorcing. It's horrible losing a parent that way, but losing your kid must be the worst."

"It's bad, Jimmy, but I wish I'd realized what a bad place it put you into. I wish I'd thought of you and tried to help you. Grief is so consuming. You can only think of yourself."

"You are helping me now. Ever since I met you I've felt better."

"I hope from now on you'll always come to me if you're feeling bad. Let me be your friend. We can go for a drive and hash it all over like we have tonight."

"Deal."

I told myself I shouldn't make promises I couldn't keep. It meant I couldn't go away to the ends of the earth, which I was set on. But Jamie, from the hood of the car, said he wanted me to stay. Stay and do what? No home, no job, no family …

"Here we are," said Jimmy, turning on to Angley's road. "What's the plan?"

"The only thing I'm sure about is that I do the returning. You don't show Angley your face or your car. I figure if I just leave the bird on his front step that will be good enough."

Soon, Jimmy parked the car. It was eleven thirty. "He's around the corner, second house. He has those lights that come on when they detect a human presence. You'll be illuminated like hell. Spotlights. It's like a mall opening."

"I remember."

"If you're not back in five minutes, I'll come to the rescue."

"No. I don't want you connected to me in any way."

"What am I supposed to do if you don't come back?"

"I don't know. I can't think. Why wouldn't I come back?"

"I can't think either." Jimmy started to laugh. He made himself stop. "How about if I follow you from a distance and watch what happens? Then I'll at least know what the deal is. I won't be sitting here, biting my nails, wondering."

"Okay. As long as you stay out of sight. And remember, we might need a quick getaway."

"If I see you running, I'll run, too."

We got the bird out of the car together then I went ahead. Except for the widely spaced streetlights, and the occasional porch light, Angley's whole street was in darkness. There was a weeping willow tree across from his house that Jimmy could blend into for an observation post. I pointed to it and he crossed the street. The house looked the same. I could see no new construction, which might denote a trap. It was the same unadorned, tan bungalow set back from the road with a cement driveway to the attached garage and a straight cement walkway to the door where the glass had been repaired. The same pathetic strips of lawn framed the walkway, no hedges or flowers, but all redeemed by the excellent grapefruit tree, the yellow globes hanging there big as blimeys.

If I kept to the walkway, I figured I wouldn't fall through a possible hole in the lawn. The lights would go on when I approached the house, alarming the man within, but I'd quickly leave the bird by the door and run like hell to the car.

It seemed simple and straightforward. Why had I fallen for the Trap Threat, which was doubtless more mis-reporting by the newspaper? Then I heard a raspy voice from behind me, from the street. "I gotcha! Walk on ahead of me with your hands up, boy. You put your hands up, too, Mister."

I turned to see Angley marching Jimmy across the street. He had a rifle. Jimmy was carrying a folding chair. "He was waiting there under the tree. Tim. He had this chair and a cooler and everything. He's probably been living there the past week."

Angley, himself, was the trap.

I set the flamingo on the ground by my legs. "Mr. Angley, I can explain everything."

"You can explain it to the police."

"But we are returning the bird. There's no need for the police. Here it is."

Did Angwin, town of two thousand souls, have a policeman? He would have to call Calistoga or St. Helena. That gave us time. But, for Jimmy's sake, it was better to persuade him not to call the police at all — second offense.

"Put the chair here," Angley said to Jimmy, gesturing to a spot outside the perimeter of where his sensor lights would come on.

When Jimmy unfolded it, he quickly sat down. Because of his back, it was probably uncomfortable for him to stand too long. "Now, go stand over there in back of your partner," he told Jimmy — partners in crime was the implication.

I understood that he wouldn't take us into his house because he didn't want Jimmy to see his furnishings and then spread the word about his bizarre penchant for large shiny animals.

Holding the rifle in the crook of his arm, he took out a cell phone, littler than Betsy's. I felt I had to stop him at once. What could be easier than disarming an old hunchback in a folding chair? A fragile, aluminum, folding chair!

This was not the FBI we'd been captured by, not a SWAT team.

At the same time, I really didn't want to get shot again. And I certainly didn't want Jimmy to get shot and prove his mother's fears to be right about our 'escapade'. And, I didn't want old Angley to get hurt either. He looked so brittle; I felt the slightest disturbance to his person would shatter his bones. I had to admire his guts, even if it was just meanness making him brave.

"Jimmy, take off. Make a run for it."

"What's the point, he's seen me."

"The point is not to get shot. Mr. Angley, please wait on that call." I simply went to the chair and took the phone from his hand. I felt bad to so belittle him by this easy move, but I misjudged him. Better I had taken the rifle from the crook of his arm. Or given the chair a kick so it would fold up again and drop him onto the lawn. "Sir ..." I began by saying as teachers loved to be called Sir, but I went no farther because the gun went off. I jumped to high heaven. The recoil caught Angley, throwing him backward, and the chair did indeed collapse so that he fell on the ground with a scream. There was also an unidentifiable pinging noise.

"Jimmy! Jimmy, are you all right?" Somehow I had got the gun in my hands. I threw it over by the garage then I, too, screamed. It was my wounded arm that threw the rifle.

"What happened?" Jimmy picked himself up from the ground where he had thrown himself and came running up to me. Lights were blinking on in all the house windows around us.

Angley snarled, "Don't touch me, and don't let any of the neighbors near my house."

People began to appear outside in bathrobes, mostly plaid.

"Shall I call an ambulance ... Sir?"

"No. I just don't want to get up right now. Get rid of those people and leave me alone."

"Jimmy, tell the neighbors everything is all right, that the gun went off by accident. Nobody hurt." Jimmy set off.

Crouching, I addressed the downed hunchback. "Mr. Angley, Jimmy had nothing to do with my taking the flamingo. I tricked him into telling me where your house was. That's all he did. I am sorry. I apologize for taking your bird and causing all of this disturbance in your life."

"Shut up."

"The reason I had to ask Jimmy the way to your house was, and please listen carefully: I did not follow you home in my car although it is true that I have a Boxster. I followed you from Petaluma, but only as far as the Angwin turnoff, Deer Park Road.".

There, I'd gotten that straight.

"I know the name of the turnoff to my own town. Go away. And take your jug ears with you."

A low blow. And I'd been so thoughtful about never mentioning his hump.

'Now, Sir, if you don't let Jimmy off the hook, and tell his father you were wrong about him, I'm letting all the neighbors into your house right now. I'll ask them to help me get you up and we will all traipse in, carrying you."

"You win," he said bitterly. I felt like a rat but just a smallish rat.

I could see Jimmy approach the various people, standing alone or in knots, to tell them they could go back to bed. Some of them were enjoying looking at the stars, which they probably hadn't noticed for a while, like since they were kids, because of television and curtains.

"Mr. Angley, please let me help you up."

"No."

"I can't just leave you here." I felt so frustrated; I wanted to kick him.

Jimmy returned. "Tim, look, the flamingo's head was shot off." He handed me the head, looking terribly pleased.

"My bird!" Angley wailed. It was a real wail, a cry of true anguish. Strange and sad it was to me, how the man had such feelings for inanimate objects, but not for humans, not for a young boy.

"Mr. Angley, even though you shot the bird that we were returning to you safe and sound, I am going to send you a check for the price you paid for both birds. And I hope that will put an end to the matter and that you will never mention Jimmy's part in this to his dad or to anyone."

"My birds!" he wailed. Plural now. He was probably putting himself in the mind of the inseparable other flamingo, thinking how she'd feel about her mate's head being blown off. If she were like Stella, she wouldn't care.

I felt really exasperated that he wouldn't get up — passive aggression at its worst. The irascible hunchback had to be aggressive no matter what he was doing, even when laying on the ground. "Sir, the damp can't be good for you. Please let Jimmy and I help you up. Do you think something is broken?"

"If you touch me, I'll kill you."

"Then I'm calling the ambulance, you idiot."

Hearing me punch in the numbers, he scrambled up quick as a monkey. "Get out of here. Get off my property."

We got. A typical Return.

XXI

FEVER

"I can't believe he really shot at us!" Jimmy kept saying. "Over a flamingo! He has to be crazy."

"That's what people do these days. Shoot. They all have guns. It's a sad time we live in."

We were on our way home. I felt awful. Now that I had got us safely away, I was falling to pieces. I was shaking. My teeth were chattering. I felt freezing cold. Jimmy didn't notice, being so excited, plus he was keeping his eyes on the road like the good driver/talker he was. I found a coat on the back seat and draped it around me. Then I was too hot. My head swam. Flashing visions of guns, flamingoes, and women, the three major food groups, dizzied me further.

When he calmed down, I tried to make a plan of what to tell his mom about our 'escapade', but my mind was useless. My wound was killing me. My head was thumping. I had marshaled my forces when I needed to and it had taken every ounce of what strength remained after this horrendous four, no FIVE, flamingo day.

"It is important not to lie," I told Jimmy, with big sighs between the words. "Once you have a reputation for stealing and lying, it is twice as hard to be believed. So you have to make a vow never to lie from now on, especially not to your mother, and keep to your vow so you can clean up your rep."

This was good stuff, but it was utter nonsense. Who of us can go a day without lying, especially to our mother and, later, our wife.

"Right. Yeah. Okay. I got it."

"Best thing would be I tell your mother the true story from the beginning."

"But then she probably won't let me see you any more," he said anxiously, warming my withered heart, "because then *you'll* have a bad rep with her. You told her we were going to confront Mr. Angley," he said, surprisingly firmly, sensing correctly that he should take the reins at this point, probably because he could feel me shaking or hear my teeth clacking. "So, that is what we'll say we did, which we did do, and we will tell her that he has the flamingo back and everything's cool and that Angley knows I'm not to blame, which I'm not."

"Except that you told her you didn't have the flamingo when you did have the flamingo," I said, feeling proud that my mind was being momentarily acute.

"Forget that," he said, continuing to take charge of the what-to-tell-mom-plan, deep down knowing that I was gaga, that my brief moment of acuity wasn't worth the brain it had come from. "Angley has the flamingo now and that's the fact we keep stressing."

I struggled to be the intelligent, concerned adult of the two of us. "She's going to want to know who took it from him and she knows about the flamingo mug and the toothpick holder."

"The whats?"

I tried to tell him, but he didn't follow me. I could hardly follow myself. Simply forming the words was a gigantic strain (especially the words toothpick and holder) as my tongue and teeth weren't connecting with my backbone or hipbone. I felt the worst kind of drunk. In the end I don't know what we decided to tell his mom because I either fell asleep or passed out. The rest of the ride I went in and out of consciousness. Sometimes I'd awaken to hear Jimmy talking. Sometimes I'd even awaken to hear me talking. I remember telling him about the blimeys then asking him if he liked fruit, telling him I wanted to be his fruit professor and teach him all I knew about fruit, and that I wanted him to be my main blimey-man.

"Cool," he said. Or maybe, "Fool."

When I next awoke, Jimmy was half carrying me, half dragging me, into his house. Lisa was saying she had been worried sick. There was a barrage of questions, which Jimmy ignored. He was going to be very good with women when he grew up.

"Help me get him to the couch, Mom. He's been shot."

This had definitely not been in the What-To-Tell-Mom-Plan as I remembered it, although it was true, I had been shot.

Physically slight though they both were, they got me couch-ward. It was wonderful to stretch out. To her exclamatory cries and continuing cannonade of questions, he simply said, "Mr. Angley shot at him."

Also true. Still …

But Jimmy was keeping to his vow of truth, sort of, and I could see that these sharp, declarative, rather shocking sentences were a good way of dealing with his highly vocal mom, whose words in anger were strung to-gether in such a way and at such a pitch, I couldn't make them out. They could have been Japanese. Had he told her yet that Angley had the fla-mingo back? That was what we were to stress, as the plan stood, to my recollection.

"Call up Mr. Angley if you don't believe me," he shouted. "Go ahead. Call him up and ask him."

Call and ask Angley if he shot me? Was this a good idea? Wasn't Jimmy getting bogged down in this shot business? Should I tell her that Mrs. Stein (I couldn't remember her first name) shot me yesterday, not Mr.

Angley today? But then she would want to know, like everyone else, if Mrs. Stein and I were lovers, and for how long.

The important thing was that Jimmy had seized the offense and he was good. But his mother was better, and her interrogative style would wear down the spunkiest boy. I knew I should come to his aid, but I was like a man in a coma who can hear but can't speak or move. Although he parried her questions, he was beginning to lose the slim edge of truthfulness he was clinging to. I hoped he wouldn't tell her once again to call the hunchback.

"Angley has the flamingo just like Tim said he did. And he knows I'm not to blame for any of it. The flamingo has been returned and I was not the one who took it."

Excellent. A plus.

Lisa said, and I understood her perfectly now, "Why did Tim go all the way to Angwin with you? It's fishy. I know he's involved."

"Tim wanted to clear my name with Mr. Angley and didn't know where he lived so that's why I had to go with him."

"Why was he so sure Mr. Angley had the flamingo? I don't get it."

"I don't know, but he did have it, so Tim was right."

This was a deliberate straying from the truth except that it was true that Angley had *A* flamingo, the other one of the pair. We had *The* flamingo.

"You see, Jimmy, what you don't know is that Tim is sort of fascinated by flamingoes. Angley's isn't the only one he's taken. I don't want to accuse him because he doesn't really steal them, more like borrows them, but ..."

Worn out and unable to act angry since his mother had now calmed down and was being thoughtful, Jimmy started to cry. It wrenched my heart, but for the life of me I still couldn't speak or even gesture. Just as well, because his tears had a beneficial effect. His mother hugged him. The boy was brilliant, really, a master.

"Tim is probably dying while you ask me all these stupid questions," he sobbed, "but what do you care?"

"Oh dear, you're right. I'll call 911."

"No, call his brother. His brother's a doctor and lives in Mill Valley."

"It's one thirty in the morning."

"He's Tim's brother and Tim's dying!"

"Okay, okay."

"And call Tim's wife, too. I think she should know he's dying – even though things aren't so great between them"

"But how do I explain his being here at my house?"

Lisa had gone from accusing Jimmy to utterly relying on him. "Don't forget," she sort of whispered, "I'm the mother of the boy who ..."

"Don't forget I'm the actual boy who ..."

Then I stopped hearing things. When I next came to, I seemed to be at George's. He was sitting by my bed. He didn't see me open my eyes because at that moment Stella was walking into the room and he looked up at her arrival. Again, it was like I was in a coma, hearing but unable to respond, a nice state of being, really. I closed my eyes.

"I can't believe it," Stella said. "I hear he's been shot again! Twice in two days. Most people go their whole lives without being shot. And by another woman. At least it was a woman who called me. She said he was here. Oh, poor darling, look at him. Is he all right?" I felt her hands tenderly touch my face, smooth my brow. I felt the mattress adjust as she sat on the bed. Astonishingly, she said, "If anything happens to Tim, I'll kill myself."

"He's running a very high fever. I've got an IV in him as you can see. He'll be all right."

"Let's put him in the hospital. I'm not taking any chances."

"This is better. I'm here watching him. Trust me. He's okay. None of his wounds are infected."

"What woman shot him this time? Was she a fat woman? A friend of mine thought she saw him in San Anselmo with a fat woman, carrying a flamingo, come to think of it, so it must have been Tim because, I don't know if you've noticed, but there's this flamingo theme to his recent behavior."

"That was probably Betsy."

"No, I met Betsy. She's the woman he bought the furniture from, for Joy's room. What a laugh that idea was."

"Not at all. Tim is going to be Joy's nanny."

"Really, George? But that's a great idea. He'll be so happy. Oh, if only he can be happy. That's all I want for him. But, wait, how did you meet Betsy?"

"I met her in Stinson Beach where Tim was returning a flamingo to her husband's shop?"

"Another flamingo? Was Tim having an affair with her?"

"Not really."

"I suppose you know about me and Derek."

"No."

"Tim didn't tell you? He tells you everything."

"He told me worse things. About your operation. That crushed him."

"It's my body."

"It's both-of-yours marriage."

"Well, how many affairs was Tim having? Marie, Betsy ... Who's this other woman who called me about Tim being shot?"

"He was at the house of Lisa Barnes."

"How strange. That's the mother of the kid who drove the car Jamie fell out of. Now she's shot Tim?"

"No, this is yesterday's shot. Apparently he was involved in another shooting this evening but the man missed. It was Mr. Angley of Angwin."

"George, seriously, do you think Tim has gone crazy?"

"He's lost his son, his business, and now you. Hasn't he a right to act crazy?"

"He hasn't lost me. He told me this morning he was leaving me, but he's not. I won't let him. I love him too much. And he loves me too much."

"Then why in hell don't you tell him you love him? And act like you love him?"

"Because I've been crazy, too." Her voice trembled. She was crying. "As soon as I told Tim about Derek and saw how it utterly destroyed him, I broke it off."

I opened my eyes. I reached out and took her hand in mine. Good, I could move. I brought her hand to my lips. I could be suave. I smiled at her lovingly. I could smile. I still couldn't speak. But I liked listening and hearing what I had heard: she loved me, she wanted me happy, she'd kill herself without me, she wanted me to be Joy's nanny. That was the best. She wouldn't be embarrassed to have a nanny husband. It was a long way from Juice King, but she didn't care. I didn't really trust her very far on the other statements.

I wanted to tell them all it wasn't true that the news about Derek had destroyed me. I had just wanted to vomit a little and maybe pull all my hair out. She can have ten lovers. Really. I just want her to be happy which is just what she wants for me. What better feelings can a marriage be built on, rebuilt on? But I still didn't have a voice.

Your mother is a great woman, James. Everything is all right with us now. We won't go away. We'll stick around. I will get my voice back. I'm just in shock from this incredibly long five flamingo day.

The next time I came to, the sun was shining and the birds were singing. Stella and Flintstone were in bed with me, Stella curled around my body, Flintstone astraddle my lower legs. George was asleep in his chair. Laurie was opening the bedroom door to let Jimmy in. I gave Jimmy a big smile. Where was Joy? I wanted her to meet her future husband.

Stella stretched and woke. Her beautiful eyes were full of morning light and the song of birds, full of love. It had been a while since we had awakened together and it was my fault. She kissed me tenderly. "I love you," I said silently, moving my lips.

Then Joy burst in, running around Jimmy, over to the bed. "Uncle Tim, look! She came back! Joy held up a little blob of pink before my eyes. It was Uno — my first, my premier, flamingo. So Uno would still be in my life, and free flamingo would, too. My creation. Maybe I would make more free flamingoes and spread them around in surprising places. That would keep me out of trouble or, even better, in trouble. I could stick them places people didn't want them.

I smiled to see Uno, but Jimmy, Stella, Laurie, even George (*et tu George?*) were looking at me disapprovingly, all of them understanding that I'd even fallen so low as to steal from a three-year-old child, my niece. They looked at me, knowing all, but forgiving all, because they loved me, they were my family. This is what life is.

'Uno flew home,' I tried to say but my voice had not flown home.

"Joy, this is Jimmy," George said.

She looked up at Jimmy with big eyes. "Is it Jamie? Did he come back, too?"

"No. But he knew Jamie."

Stella said it. Stella! She said Jimmy knew Jamie. It was a break-through. She was talking about Jamie to others for the first time. "He and his brother, Paul, played with Jamie a lot," she continued, still talking about Jamie. "Just like you did, Joy, honey."

"Will you play with me?" Joy asked Jimmy, who smiled, shrugged, and said, "I guess so." Already putty in her hands. "Uncle Tim is my nanny," she told him proudly. "And my 'mingo flew home fwom where he was dead."

"Flamingoes can do that," Jimmy told her, nodding seriously. "They're incredible birds. There is a mythical bird called the phoenix, which was probably the first flamingo. The phoenix never dies."

"Mythical ..." Joy struggled with the word but got it out; luckily there was no letter r in it. She smiled. "We're mythical, too. We'll never die, will we, Uncle Tim."

The End

CPSIA information can be obtained at www.ICGtesting.com
Printed in the USA
LVOW081314170213

320457LV00003B/430/P